U0052997

工業英文

許廷珪 著

三民書局

國家圖書館出版品預行編目資料

工業英文／許廷珪著.－－初版十四刷.－－臺北市：
三民，2018
    面；　公分.

    ISBN 978–957–14–1143–9　（平裝）

    1.工業英文

800

© 　工業英文

著 作 人	許廷珪
發 行 人	劉振強
著作財產權人	三民書局股份有限公司
發 行 所	三民書局股份有限公司
	地址　臺北市復興北路386號
	電話　(02)25006600
	郵撥帳號　0009998–5
門 市 部	(復北店) 臺北市復興北路386號
	(重南店) 臺北市重慶南路一段61號
出版日期	初版一刷　1975年8月
	初版十四刷　2018年5月
編 號	S 800210

行政院新聞局登記證局版臺業字第○二○○號

有著作權·不准侵害

ISBN 978–957–14–1143–9　（平裝）

http://www.sanmin.com.tw　三民網路書店
※本書如有缺頁、破損或裝訂錯誤，請寄回本公司更換。

序　言

　　近十年來台灣工業有驚人的發展，此種成就固應歸功於政府的政策領導、工廠主的苦心經營、各學術研究機構以及各工廠技術人員之努力；但無可否認的，引進美、日等先進國家技術以及仰賴國外技術合作亦為其重要關鍵。

　　目前的台灣工業正在逐漸擺脫對國外技術的依存性，邁向獨立自主開發技術之途。欲宏大其效果，必須蒐集及研讀國外技術文獻。即最起碼必須培養英文專門文獻，英文專門雜誌，工業新聞英文版，甚至型錄廣告文的閱讀能力。然而工職、工專畢業就職於有關公司、工廠後，仍無法判讀簡單圖面上的英文單字或機械的英文操作法說明，其原因在於在學校雖然每週有英文課，但其內容不涉及有關工業的英文，亦即並不教授工業英文 (Engineering English)。因此學非所用，連最簡單的專門術語 (Technical Terms) 也不會寫，更談不上專門書籍之判讀。

　　編者有鑑於此，經由工業技術研究院金屬工業研究所金屬材料科學研究室各同仁之支持與協助下，特編本教材。內容包括機械、電氣、化學、電子、土木、建築、冶金、船舶、原子能等範圍極為廣泛。確信工職、工專、大學工程系學生，以及現場的領班、技術員、中堅技術幹部，均可藉助本書在短期間內一方面能擴大對科學技術的基本知識，一方面能增強工業英文的閱讀力。

　　編者才疏學淺，又因倉促編就，內容難免多有錯誤欠妥之處，尚祈各界先進惠予指教是幸。

工學博士　許廷珪
謹識於工技院金屬工業研究所

工業英文　目錄

序　言

入　門　編

1. EASY ARITHMETIC (簡單的計算) 1
2. A CIRCLE (圓) 4
3. MEASURING TEMPERATURE (溫度的測定) 6
4. WEIGHTS and MEASURES (度量衡) 11
5. DENSITY AND SPECIFIC GRAVITY........................17
6. WATTS and KILOWATTS (瓦特及千瓦特) 21
7. OHM'S LAW (歐姆定律) 23

學　習　編

1. AN APARTMENT HOUSE (公寓) 27
2. COPPER (銅) 31
3. TANKERS (油輪) 35
4. LATHES (車床) 42
5. WHAT IS AUTOMATION? (何爲自動化) 48
6. THE ORIGIN OF THE STEAM TURBINE
   (蒸汽機之起源) 52
7. ELEMENTS AND SYMBOLS (元素與符號) 58
8. A NUCLEAR POWER PLANT (核子發電廠)................64

研 究 編

1. SAFETY PRECAUTIONS IN THE MACHINE SHOP......69
2. PRODUCING STEEL by THE BESSEMER PROCESS......73
3. INTERNAL—COMBUSTION ENGINES............76
4. MECHANICAL DRAWING 79
5. GENERATORS 84
6. TOOTHED GEARS............90
7. WELDING 97
8. THE AIRCRAFT INDUSTRY............ 104

參 考 編

1. 工業英文法的概要 119
2. 工業英文的語源研究——字首與字尾 159

附 錄

1. 美國式拼字 171
2. 美語與英語的對照比較表 173

入 門 編

1. EASY ARITHMETIC (簡單的計算)

[1] Addition

$$2+3=5$$

Two and three are five.

Two and three make five.

Two plus three equals five.

〔單語〕 easy 〔'i:zi〕 容易的。arithmetic 〔'əriθmətik〕 算數，計算。
addition 〔'ədiʃən〕 加法。make 〔meik〕 成爲……。
plus 〔plʌs〕 加……。equal 〔'i:kwəl〕 等於。

〔譯文〕 加法

$$2+3=5$$

2和3是5。

2和3成爲5。

2加3等於5。

〔解說〕 數學式子的讀法很多，但在工程上最常用的是 Two plus three equals five. make 是「成爲……」之意。 例如，Cotton makes cheap clothing. 棉布成爲便宜的衣類。

[2] Subtraction

$$10-8=2$$

Eight from ten leaves two.

Ten minus eight is two.

Ten minus eight equals two.

〔單語〕 subtraction 〔səb'trækʃən〕 減法。leave 〔li:v〕 剩下。

minus 〔'mainəs〕減去……。

〔譯文〕減法　　　　　　　$10-8=2$

從10減8剩下2

10減8是2

10減8等於2

〔解說〕工程上最常用的是最後的 Ten minus eight equals two.

即加法用 plus, 減法用 minus。

[3] Multiplication　　$4\times2=8$

Twice four is eight.

$5\times6=30$

Six times five is thirty.

Six times five make thirty.

Five multiplied by six equals thirty.

$9.5\times6=57$

Nine point five multiplied by six equals

fifty seven.

〔單語〕multiplication 〔mʌltipli'keiʃən〕乘法。twice 〔twais〕2倍。
time 〔taim〕倍。multiplied 〔'mʌltiplai〕multiply 的過去式或過去分
詞。point 〔pɔint〕小數點, 點。

〔譯文〕乘法　　　　　　$4\times2=8$

4的2倍是8

$5\times6=30$

5的6倍是30

5的6倍成爲30

5乘以6等於30

$$9.5 \times 6 = 57$$

9.5乘以 6 等於57

〔解說〕 2 倍平常不叫 two time, 而稱為 twice. 在工程上乘的時侯常說成 multiplied by～。小數點稱為 decimal point, 通常簡稱 point.

[4] Division　　　　$147 \div 6 = 24.5$

A (One) hundred and forty-seven divided by six equals twenty-four point five.

$$100/4 = 25$$

A (One) hundred over four is twenty-five.

A (One) hundred over four equals twenty-five.

〔單語〕 division 〔di'viʒən〕 除法, divided 〔di'vaidid〕 divide (除) 的過去式和過去分詞。

〔譯文〕 除法　　　$147 \div 6 = 24.5$

147除以 6 等於24.5

$100/4$

4 分之100是25

4 分之100等於25

〔解說〕 divided by～是除以～。工程上"＋"是 plus, "－"是 minus, "×"是 multipled by, "÷"是 divided by. 關於數量擬在參考編的文法「數量形容詞」中詳細說明。

〔練　習　一〕

用英文讀出下面的數式:

1. $10+7=17$　　　2. $15-11=4$　　　3. $80 \times 4 = 320$

4. $13.3+3=16.3$　　5. $80/4=20$

2. A CIRCLE （圓）

[1] The distance across a circle, through its center, is called the diameter of the circle. The distance around the circle is circumference.

〔單語〕 circle 〔ˈsəːkl〕 圓。 distance 〔ˈdistəns〕 距離。 across 〔əˈkrɔːs〕 橫過。 through 〔θruː〕 通過。 called 〔kɔːl〕 call（叫做）的過去式及過去分詞。 diameter 〔daiˈæmitə〕 直徑。 center 〔ˈsentə〕 中心。 around 〔əˈraund〕 周圍。 circumference 〔səˈkʌmfərəns〕 圓周。

〔譯文〕 橫過圓而通過其中心的距離，稱爲圓的直徑。 圓的周圍的距離稱爲圓周。

〔解說〕 through its center 通過其中心。is called～ 被稱爲～。這種形叫被動式，用〔be 動詞＋過去分詞〕表示，譯成「被……」。是工程用語常用而重要的基本形。例 This tool is called spanner.（這工具被稱爲鉗子）細節請參照文法中〔過去分詞之用法〕。the distance around the circle 圓的周圍的距離。

[2] The circumference of any circle is always the same number times the diameter.

This number cannot be written exactly as a fraction or decimal, so we use a Greek letter, π (pi), to stand for it.

It is almost equal to $3^1/_7$ or 3.1416.

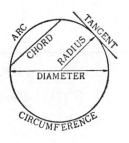

〔單語〕 always 〔ˈɔːlweis〕 總是。　same 〔seim〕 相同，同一。　**exactly** 〔egˈzæktli〕 正確地。　fraction 〔ˈfrækʃən〕 分數。　**Greek letter** 〔griːk ˈletə〕 希臘字。 π〔pai〕 希臘字的圓周率記號。radius 〔ˈreidiəs〕

半徑。chord〔kɔːd〕弦。tangent〔'tændʒənt〕切線。

〔譯文〕任何圓的圓周總是直徑的相同數的倍數。這數不能以分數或小數正確的表示。因此我們用希臘文的 π 來代表它。π 差不多等於$3^1/_7$或是3.1416。

〔解說〕any circle 任何一個圓。the same number times 相同數的倍數→同一倍數。cannot be written 不能寫出來（被動態之否定文）。stand for~ 代表~, 表示~。stand 是「站立，建立」之意。〔例〕A factory stands on a hill 一工廠建在山丘上。The thermometer stands at 90°C, 溫度計升在 90°C, 但如本文的 stand for. 加上 for 的時候成爲「代表~」「表示~」的成語，例 N stand for. the North. N 表示北。$3\frac{1}{7}$ 念 three and one-seventh, 3.1416 念 three (decimal) point one four one six.

3. *MEASURING TEMPERATURE* (溫度的測定)

[1] Temperature is measured with an instrument known as a thermometer.

　A thermometer consists of a long and very narrow glass tube with a bulb at the one end.

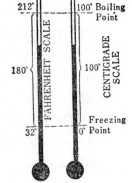

〔單語〕measuring 〔'meʒəriŋ〕測定 (動名詞)。

　　　　temperature 〔'tempritʃə〕溫度。

　　　　instrument 〔'instrumənt〕器具，儀器。

　　　　thermometer 〔θə'mɔmitə〕溫度計。consist of~ 〔kən'sist ɔf〕由 …作成，由~成立。narrow 〔'nærou〕狹的，細的。tube 〔tju:b〕管。 bulb 〔bʌlb〕球。end 〔end〕末端，終點。

〔譯文〕溫度是以一種器具卽大家所知道的溫度計來測定。溫度計是由在一端附 有一個球的長而細的玻璃管作成。

〔解說〕measuring 是動詞 measeure (測定) 的現在分詞，在此地用作動名詞， 因此譯成「溫度的測定」而不是測定溫度。is measured 被測定 (被動 態)。known as ~ 大家知道的，已知的，有名的 consist 常附有 of 〔例〕This machine consists of three parts 這機器由三個部分作成。 with a bulb 附有球，narrow glass tube 細玻璃管。at one end 在 一端。

[2] Inside the bulb and tube there is a silvery liquid called mercury. There are two temperature scales, centigrade and fahrenheit.

〔單語〕silvery 〔'silvəri〕銀色的。mercury 〔'mə:kjuri〕水銀。

scale 〔skeil〕 刻度，度數。centigrade 〔'sentigreid〕 攝氏。
fahrenheit 〔'færənhait〕 華氏。

〔譯文〕 球及管裡面有被稱爲水銀的銀色液體，有兩種溫度的刻度，攝氏及華氏。

〔解說〕 centigrade 溫度計的攝氏，略字爲 C，有100分度之意。
fahrenhite 溫度計的華氏，略字爲 F 或 Fahr.

[3] In the centigrade scale, denoted as °C., the freezing point of
water is called 0°C., and the boiling point of water is called 100°C.

〔單語〕 denoted 〔dinoutid〕 denote（表示）的過去，過去分詞。　　degree
〔di'gri:〕度數。freezing 〔'frizin〕 freeze（凍結）的現在分詞 boiling
〔'bɔilin〕 boil（沸騰）的現在分詞。

〔譯文〕 以 C 度表示的攝氏刻度之中，水的氷點被稱爲 0°C，而水的沸點被稱
爲 100°C。

〔解說〕 centigrade scale C 刻度，攝氏刻度。denoted as 以…表示的（＝
which is denoted as～）。freezing point 氷點（freezing 具有形容
詞的作用，凍結的點──→氷點）。boiling point 沸點（沸騰的點──
沸點）。100°C 唸成 one hundred degrees C 或 centigrade.

[4] Thus, this scale has 100 degrees between the two standard
points. The centigrade scale is used in all scientific work.

〔單語〕 between 〔bi'twin〕 在…之間。　　standard 〔'stændəd〕 基準，標準。
scientific 〔saiən'tifik〕 科學（上）的。

〔譯文〕 如此，這刻度在兩個基準點之間有 100 度，攝氏刻度使用在所有科學上
的工作。

〔解說〕 between 用於表示二者之間。〔例〕 between A and B──→AB 之間

science 科學。work 動詞時是操作，勞動之意，名詞時是工作，工作物。

[5] In the fahrenheit scale, denoted °F., the freezing point of water is called 32°F., and the boiling point of water is called 212°F.

Thus, in this scale there are 180 degrees between the two standard points.

〔單語〕 F:fahrenheit 〔ˈfærənhait〕 華氏之略字。

〔譯文〕 以 F 度表示的 F 刻度，水的冰點被稱爲 32°F，而水的沸點被稱爲 212°F。如此，此種刻度在兩個基準點間有 180 度。

〔解說〕 denoted=which is denoted 之意。32°F 讀成 thirty-two F. (或 fahrenheit)。212°F 讀成 two hundred and twelve degrees F.。

[6] The fahrenheit scale is used in the home and industry. The two temperature scales are related by the following expression:

$$°F.=9/5°C.+32$$

〔單語〕 industry 〔ˈindʌstri〕 產業，工業。 related 〔riˈleitid〕 relate (有關係) 的過去，過去分詞。 following 〔ˈfɔlouiŋ〕 後面的，以下的。expression 〔eksˈpreʃən〕 表現，表示法。

〔譯文〕 F 刻度用於家庭及工業上，這兩種溫度刻度相互關係以下式表示。

$$°F.=9/5°C.+32$$

〔解說〕 industry 是產業，工業。iron industry 鐵工業。are related (被動) 有關，文中的 related by 可譯成符合，滿足。following expression 下面的表示。〔例〕 following formula 下面的公式，following example 以下的例題。°F=9/5°C.+32 讀成 degree F equals nine-fifths degree C plus thirty-two.

[7] This expression can be used to convert degrees fahrenheit into degrees centigrade and vice versa.

〔單語〕 convert 〔kən'vəːt〕 變換，換算。vice versa 〔'vaisi 'vəːsə〕 反過來也是一樣。

〔譯文〕 這表示法能够用來把華氏換算爲攝氏以及反過來也一樣（把攝氏換算成華氏也一樣）。

〔解說〕 can be used 能被用於→能用於（can use 之被動態）。to convert~ into~ 爲了把…變換爲…。vice versa 拉丁語的反過來，其反面也一樣之意。

〔練　習　二〕

（A）　用英文讀出下面的溫度

80°F.　155°F.　18°C.　98°C.

（B）　翻譯下面的英文

(1) Temperature is measured either in fahrenheit or in centigrade.

（either~or 或…或…，不是…就是…）

(2) On the centigrade scale the freezing point is at zero, and the boiling point is at 100°

（zero 零，0）

(3) While on the fahrenheit scale the freezing point is at 32°, and the boiling point 212°

（while 當……，另一方面……）

（C）　用英文寫出下面的句子。

(1) 在F刻度沸點記成212°

(2) 另一方面在C刻度沸點記成100°

（記成 mark〔mɑ:k〕）

有關溫度計的術語

air thermometer	空氣溫度計
centigrade thermometer	攝氏溫度計
dial〔'daiəl〕thermometer	指針盤溫度計
fahrenheit thermometer	華氏溫度計
mercury thermometer	水銀溫度計
thermometry〔θə:'mɔmitri〕	溫度測定

4. WEIGHTS and MEASURES （度量衡）

【1】 There are two basic systems of units for weights and measures;
——— One is the Metric System, and the other is the English
System.

The Metric System is now the accepted system in all scientific
work in all countries.

〔單語〕 weights and measures 〔weits and ′medʒəz〕度量衡。basic 〔′beisik〕
基本的。system 〔′sistim〕方式，制度。metric 〔′metrik〕公尺制的。
unit 〔′juːnit〕單位。accepted 〔æ′kseptid〕被公認。

〔譯文〕 關於度量衡有兩種基本單位方式。一種是公制而另一種是英國制。
公尺制是現在所有各國在科學工作上被公認的制度。

〔解說〕 weights and measures 習慣上用複數形。for～ 用法很多，此地指關
於～，說到～。basic system of units 基本的單位方式。the Metric
System 公尺制。the English system 英國制。accepted 是 (accept)
的過去過去分詞，但在此地是形容詞用法。名詞是 acceptance 公認。
in all countries: 在所有各國。

Length （長度）

【2】 The fundamental length of unit in Metric System is the
standard meter The following table gives the most commonly
used Metric units of length. Notice that the name of each is
formed by putting a distinguishing prefix to the word "Meter."

〔單語〕 length 〔leŋθ〕長度。fundamental 〔fʌndə′mentəl〕基本的，根本的。
meter 〔′miːtə〕公尺 (=metre)。　　table 〔teibl〕表。　　commonly

〔'kɔmənli〕通常，一般。notice〔'noutis〕注意。that〔ðæt〕連接詞，用在名詞子句的開頭，這種 that 口語中常常省去不說。 form〔fɔ:m〕造成，作成。putting〔putiŋ〕put（放置）的動名詞。distinguishing〔dis'tiŋgwiʃiŋ〕區別 distinguish 的現在分詞 prefix〔'prifiks〕接頭語。

〔譯文〕公尺制的基本長度單位是標準公尺，下表表示出通常最常用的公尺制長度單位。注意各自的名稱係在"公尺"附上可區別的接頭語而成。

〔解說〕following table 次表。most commonly used Metric units 最普通常用的公尺制單位。used 是 use（用）的過去，過去分詞，在此地有形容詞的作用。notice that 注意……的事（在此地 that 是連接詞，不要誤用為關係代名詞）

〔例〕(a) I think *that* he is a painter 我想他是塗裝工（連接詞，painter〔'peintə〕塗裝工。

(b) This is the machine *that* I made 這是我所作的機械（關係代名詞）

is formed 形成的→所作的。 by putting 靠附上（動名詞）。distinguishing prefix 可區別的接頭語。distinguishing 有形容詞的作用。the word "meter"「公尺」這個字。

【3】 For instance, a centimeter is 0.01 meter, and a kilometer is 1,000meters. The standard abbreviations and the relations to the English system are also given.

Table 1. Metric Units of Length

1 kilometer (km)　=1,000meters

1 METER (m)　=PRIMARY UNITS

1 centimeter (cm)　=0.01 meter

1 millimeter (mm)　=0.001 meter

1 km = 0.621 mile.　1m= 39.4 in.　2.54cm = 1 in.

〔單語〕instance〔'instəns〕例，實例。 centimeter〔'sentimi:tə〕厘米（略字 cm）。 kilometer〔'kiləmi:tə〕公里（略字 km）。 abbreviation〔əbri:vi'eiʃən〕略語，略字。 relation〔ri'leiʃən〕關係。 primary〔'praiməri〕基本的（＝basic）。 millimeter〔'milimi:tə〕毫米（略字 mm）。 km＝kilometer 的略字。 in＝inch〔intʃ〕英吋的略字。

〔譯文〕例如，1厘米等於0.01公尺，1公里等於1000公尺，對英制的基本略字及其關係列舉於下。

表1　公尺制長度單位表。

1公里（km）＝1000公尺（m）

1公尺（m）＝基本單位

1厘米（cm）＝0.01公尺（m）

1毫米（mm）＝0.001公尺

1公里（km）＝0.621英哩

1公尺（m）＝39.4英吋

2.45厘米（cm）＝1英吋

〔解說〕for instance（＝for example）例如。 primary unit（＝basic unit）基本單位。are given 列舉於下（被動式）

AREA AND VOLUME（面積和體積）

【4】For area measurement we have square inches, square feet, square centimeters, square kilometers, etc. Square centimeters is witten cm^2, square inches is in^2, and so on, but these abbreviation are to be read as "square centimeters" and "square inches".

〔單語〕area〔'ɛəriə〕面積。　Volume〔'va(ɔ)ljum〕容積，體積。 measurement〔'meʒəmənt〕測定。 square〔skwɛə〕平方的。

〔譯文〕對於面積測量有平方英吋，平方英尺，平方厘米，平方公里等。平方厘

米可寫爲 cm^2 平方英吋寫爲 in^2 以此類推。但這些略字讀做平方厘米，平方英吋。

〔解說〕We have 有（＝There are）。　square inch 平方英吋。　square kilometer 平方公里。　is written 被寫爲。are to be read as～被讀做。

【5】 Volume requires a cubical unit for its measurement. Thus these are cubic centimeters (cm^3), cubic feet (ft^3), etc. In all, volume measurement goes very much like length and area measurement.

〔單語〕require 〔ri'kwaiə〕需要。cubical 〔'kju:bik〕立方的。

〔譯文〕體積的測定需要一種立方體的單位，於是有立方厘米，立方英呎等。總之，體積的測量與長度和面積的測量極爲相似。

〔解說〕a cubical unit 立方體的單位。　cubic centimeter 立方厘米。cubic feet 立方英呎。in all 總之，卽。goes very much like 非常相似。

【6】 There is a special name given to a Metric unit of volume equal to 1,000 cm^3. It is called a liter, and is just larger than a liquid quart.

〔單語〕special 〔'speʃəl〕特別的。　liter 〔'li:tə〕（＝ litre）公升。liquid 〔'likwid〕液體。　quart 〔kwɔ:t〕夸特（＝$\frac{1}{4}$加侖）。

〔譯文〕體積的公尺制單位有一個特殊名詞等於 1000cm^3，它被稱爲 1 公升，比 1 夸特僅多一點點。

〔解說〕a special name (which is) given to 特殊的名稱對…。is just larger than 比…僅多一點。liquid quart 爲液體計量的單位。

Mass（質量）

[7] The fundamental Metric standard of mass is the kilogram, a cylinder of platinum alloy kept at the international Bureau of Weights and Measures.

Table 2 gives the commoner Metric mass Unit, their abbreviations, and how they are related to the English units.

〔單語〕mass 〔mæs〕質量。kilogram 〔ˈkiləgræm〕（＝kilogramme）公斤。
　　　platinum 〔ˈplætinəm〕白金。　　alloy 〔əˈlɔi〕合金。
　　　international 〔intəˈnæʃənəl〕國際的。　bureau 〔ˈbjuːrou〕局，科。
　　　commoner〔ˈkɔmənə〕common 的比較級（＝more common）通常的。

〔譯文〕質量的基本公尺制單位是公斤，以一個放在國際度量衡標準局裡的白金
　　　圓柱體作爲標準。
　　　表2，表示較常用的公尺制的質量單位，他們的略字，以及與英制
　　　的相互關係。

〔解說〕kept＝which is kept 保存在……。
　　　International Bureau of Weights and Measures 國際度量衡標準局。
　　　how they are related to～ 與……有怎樣的關係。

[8] Table 2. Metric Units of Mass
1 Metric ton ＝1,000 kilograms
1 kilogram（kg）　＝PRIMARY UNIT
1 gram（gm）　＝0.001 kg
1 milligram（mg）　＝0.001 gm
1 kg ＝2.2 lb, 454gm ＝1 lb, 1 oz＝28.4 gm

〔單語〕milligram 〔'miligræm〕毫克（＝milligramme）。

lb（＝pound〔paund〕的略字）磅。　　oz（＝ounce〔auns〕的略字）重量單位，盎斯。

【練　習　三】

用英文寫出下文:

1. 1英吋等於2.54厘米。

2. 工程上的單位全都根據公尺制

工程上的單位 engineering unit 根據…be based on

3. 公尺制的度量衡使用於所有科學上的工作。

Metric Prefixes（公尺制接頭語）

Used With Basic Units: Meter, Liter, Gram

milli-	0.001
centi-	0.01
deci-	0.1
deka-	10
hecto-	100
kilo-	1000

Used with Basic Unit; Meter, Liter, Gram.（基本單位: 與公尺・公升・公克一起使用）。

5. DENSITY AND SPECIFIC GRAVITY

[1] Density is the weight of a unit volume of a substance. This is usually expressed as g./cc. in the Metric system, or lbs/cu.ft. in the Englisg system.

〔單語〕 density 〔'densiti〕 密度。specific 〔spi'sifik〕 特殊的，特有的。gravity 〔'græviti〕 重力。　weight 〔weit〕 重量。　substance 〔'səbstəns〕 物質。　usually 〔'juːʒuəli〕 普通，一般。　expressed 〔eks'presid〕 express (表達) 的過去式，過去分詞。

〔譯文〕 密度是一物質單位體積的重量。通常在公尺制裡以 g/cc，或在英制裡以 lbs/cu.ft. 表示。

〔解說〕 g/cc 單位表示每 1cc 的物質重若干克 (grams per cubic centimeter)。lbs/cu.ft. 單位表示每 1 立方英尺的物質重若干磅 (pounds per cubic foot)。specific gravity 比重。usually 是副詞，而其形容詞爲 usual (普通的)。is expressed as~以…表達 (被動式)。

[2] Since 1 cc. of water weighs 1 gm., its density is 1 g./cc. A cubic foot of water weighs 62.4 lbs. The density of water in the English system is 62.4 lbs/ft^3.

〔單語〕 since 〔sins〕 因爲…

〔譯文〕 因爲 1cc 水重 1g，水的密度是 1g/cc。1 立方英呎的水重62.4磅。水的密度在英制爲62.4 lbs/cu.ft.

〔解說〕 since 是連接詞，其功用在於連接。1cc of water weighs 1g (水 1cc 重 1g) 所以 Its density is 1g/cc (其密度是1g/cc)，比 because 語氣稍弱，比 as 或 for 爲較正式的說法。62.4 lbs/cu,ft. 讀成 sixty-two point four pounds per cubic foot 意思是62.4磅每立方英呎。

【3】 Multiplying a metric density by 62.4 gives the English density of the substance. The following table shows densities of some common substances.

Substances	g./cc.	lbs./cu. ft.
aluminum	2.7	168.5
copper	8.9	555.4
gold	19.3	1204.3
ice	0.917	57.2
mercury	13.6	849.0
lead	11.3	705.1
water, fresh	1.0	62.4
water, sea	1.025	64.0

〔單語〕 aluminum 〔æ′lju: minəm〕 鋁, (英式 aluminium 〔æ′ljuminiən〕)。 copper 〔′kɑ(ɔ)pə〕 銅。 gold 〔gould〕 金。 ice 〔ais〕 水。 lead 〔led〕 鉛。 fresh 〔freʃ〕 純粹的。

〔譯文〕 公尺制單位的密度乘以 62.4即爲英制單位的密度，下表表示某些常用物質的密度。

〔解說〕 multipling～by～以…乘以～, multipling 是動名詞。

【4】 Specific gravity is the ratio of the weight of a given volume of a substance to the weight of the same volume of water at the same temperature.

〔單語〕 ratio 〔′reiʃou〕 比, 比率。

〔譯文〕 比重是在同溫時，一定體積的物質的重量與同體積水的重量比。

〔解說〕 a given volume: 所給的體積, given 是 give 的過去分詞，但在此

地當作形容詞,〔例〕given value. 所給的值→已知值。

required power 所求的動力→所需的動力。

as substance to~的 to 是「對~」的意思的前置詞。

[5] Since 1 cc. of water weighs 1 g., specific gravity is numerically equal to the metric density of a substance.

Both density and specific gravity have to do with the "lightness" or "heaviness" of a substance.

〔單語〕numerically 〔nju:'merikəli〕數式的, 在數字上。

　　　　lightness 〔'laitnis〕輕。　　　　heaviness 〔'hevinis〕重。

〔譯文〕因為 1cc 水重 1g。比重和公尺制的密度在數字上相等。

　　　　密度和比重二者都與物質的輕或重有關。

〔解說〕is equal to~ 等於。　have to do with~ 與……有關。　heaviness 是形容詞 heavy 的名詞, 同樣 lightness 是 light 的名詞。

[6] Aluminum is "lighter" than lead. Water is "lighter" than mercury. Density is used more with solids, while specific gravity is used more with liquids or solutions.

〔單語〕lighter 〔'laitə〕light (輕)的比較級。　solution 〔sə'lju:ʃən〕溶液。

〔譯文〕鋁比鉛輕, 水比水銀輕。密度多用於固體, 而比重多用於液體或溶液。

〔解說〕is used more: 多用於。with solid 的 with 不是「與…」而有「於…, 關於…」的意思。while 是「另一方面, 相反的」等有對立的意思。solution 除了「溶液」外另有「解答」的意思。

〔練　習　四〕

翻譯下面的英文:

1. How many cc. of cork will weigh the same as 1 cc. of gold?

2. The acid in a car battery has a specific gravity of 1.28 when the battery is fully charged.

   acid〔ˊæsid〕酸。car battery〔kɑː ˊbætəri〕汽車用蓄電池。

   fully〔ˊfuli〕完全的，十分的。charge〔tʃɑːdʒ〕充電。

3. Which substances in the above table will float on water?

   the above table 上表

6. WATTS and KILOWATTS（瓦特及千瓦特）

〔1〕 Watt is a unit for measuring power, especially electric power. One watt is the power of a current of one ampere flowing under an E.M.F. of one volt.

〔單語〕 watt 〔wɑ(ɔ)t〕 瓦特，（電力單位）。 killowatt 千瓦特（＝1000瓦特）。 especially 〔es'peʃəli〕 尤其是，特殊的。 electric 〔i'lektrik〕 電的。 ampere 〔'æmpɛə〕 安培（電流的強度單位）。 flowing 〔flouiŋ〕 flow（流量）的動名詞及現在分詞。 　　　　　E.M.F electromotive force 〔i'lektroumoutiv fɔ:s〕 即電動勢的略字。volt 〔voult〕 伏特（電壓的實用單位）。

〔譯文〕 瓦特是用以測量動力的單位，尤其是電功率，一瓦特就是一安培的電流在電動勢為 1 伏特之下流動，而產生的功率。

〔解說〕 watt 即瓦特，這單位的擬定，係由蒸氣機的發明始祖 James Watt 所創，故取其名。for measuring～ 用以測定…（動名詞）動名詞通常附有前置詞。不定詞 to measure 也相同。（例）A scale is an instrument for measuring the length. 量尺是一種用以量測長度的器具。electric power 電力。flowing 流動（說明 ampere 的形容詞用法）。under……之下。

〔2〕 A watt is also equal to about 44 foot-pounds per minute.

watts＝volts×amperes

746 watts＝1 horsepower

Kilowatt is a unit for measuring power equal to 1,000 watts. Often abbreviated Kw.

1 kilowatt＝1,000 watts 　　　1 kilowatt＝ 1.34 horsepower

〔單語〕foot-pound〔'fut-paund〕呎—磅。horse-power〔'hɔ:spauə〕馬力
（略字爲 hp. H.P. IP.）。abbreviated〔ə'brivieitid〕abbreviate（省
略）的過去式及過去分詞。kw. kilowatt 的略字。

〔譯文〕一瓦特也等於每分鐘44呎—磅的能量。

瓦特＝伏特×安培

746瓦特＝１馬力

千瓦特是量度相當於1000瓦特之功率時所用之單位。常被縮寫爲 kw.

1 千瓦特＝1000瓦特 　　　1 千瓦特＝1.34 馬力

〔解說〕is equal to 相當於，等於。44 foot-pounds per minute 每分鐘44
呎—磅的能量。foot-pounds (ft-lb.) 係英制單位公尺制是 kilogram-
meter (kg-m²) watts＝volts×amperes 讀成 watts equals volts
multiplied by amperes. kilo—是 1000 的接頭語。〔例〕kilocycle (kc)
kilovolt (kv). Often abbreviated kw. 是 It is often abbreviated
as kw 之意。

7. OHM'S LAW (歐姆定律)

[1] The current (in amperes) flowing in any circuit is equal to the electromotive force (in volts) divided by the resistance (in ohms). This relationship is expressed in three formulas:

$$I=\frac{E}{R} \qquad R=\frac{E}{I} \qquad E=IR$$

〔單語〕 Ohm's 〔oumz〕 歐姆氏 的 (人名)。 law 〔lɔ:〕 定律。
current 〔'kə:rənt〕 電流。 circuit 〔'sə:kit〕 電路, 回路。
resistance 〔ri'zistəns〕 電阻。 ohm 〔oum〕 歐姆 (卽電阻之單位)
relationship 〔ri'leiʃənʃip〕 關係。

〔譯文〕 在任一電路內流動的電流 (以安培表之) 等於電動勢 (以伏特表之) 除
以電阻 (以歐姆表之)。此關係可寫成下列三式:

$$I=\frac{E}{R} \qquad R=\frac{E}{I} \qquad E=IR$$

〔解說〕 Ohm's Law 歐姆定律, 係德國人歐姆氏 (George Simon Ohm) 於
1827年所創定之電壓電流與電阻間之關係式。名詞的所有格加上相當與
「…的」 的 ~'s。〔例〕 Mr. Hsu's book 許先生的書。sun's ray 太陽
的光線。current 電流, 卽 electric current。resistance 電阻, 卽
electric resistance。formulas 又可寫爲 formulae 〔'fɔmjuli:〕 爲
formula 之複數。I=E/R 讀成 I equals E by (或over) R.

[2] In these three formulas, I stands for the Intensity of the current flow in amperes, E stands for the Electromotive force in volts, and R stands for the Resistance in ohms.

〔單語〕Intensity〔in'tensity〕強度。flow〔flou〕流量（名詞）。

〔譯文〕在這三個公式中，I 表以安培爲單位之電流量之强度，E 表以伏特爲單
位之電動勢，R 表以歐姆爲單位之電阻。

〔解說〕stand for 代表，表示。〔例〕What does this sign stand for? 這記
號代表什麼意思。in ampere's 用安培。in millimeter 用毫米。

〔練 習 五〕

翻譯下面的英文:

1. As you know, the formulas of Ohm's law express the relation
   between rate of current flow, E.M.F., and resistance.

   As you know 如已知 rate 比率

2. The power of electric motors is often stated in horsepower; therefore
   it is sometimes necessary to change the horsepower to watts or
   kilowatts.

   electric motor〔i'lektrik 'moutə〕電動馬達。stated〔steitid〕state（敍述）
   之過去式及過去分詞。therefore〔'ðɛəfɔə〕因此

電氣用術語之研究

庫倫 coulomb〔kú:lɔm〕（略字C）。 Coulomb 氏制定的電量實用單位，
Coulomb 氏又以庫倫定律（Coulomb's law）聞名。

安培 ampere（略字 amp. 或 A）電流的實用單位。1 秒中以 1 庫倫之比率
流動的電流强度。法國人 Ampere 氏之名爲單位名。

電流（electric current）電流繼續在導體 Conductor 內流動的現象，卽電
位 electric potential 不同的二物體用導線連接時電 electricity 在導體內移動，
以正電 positive electricity 移動的方向爲電流的方向。

伏特 volt（略字V）。電壓 voltage 的實用單位。1 歐姆之電阻下使 1 安培
之電流流動所需的電位差 potential difference（電壓）稱爲 1 伏特。取自意大

利物理學家 Volta 之名。

　　歐姆 ohm（略字 Ω ）電阻之單位。在導體之二點間加上 1 伏特的電位差而發生 1 安培之電流時，此二點間的電阻為 1 歐姆，取自德國人 Ohm 氏之名。

　　電動勢 electromotive force（略字 E.M.F. 或 e.m.f）在二物體間使之產生電位差的作用，或在電氣回路上使電流流動的驅動力。

學 習 編

1. AN APARTMENT HOUSE (公寓)

【1】 My home is in an apartment house. I live high up in a concrete building as tall as the tallest tree of the forest.

〔單語〕apartment house 〔ə'pɑːtmənt haus〕公寓，共同住宅。　concrete 〔kɔnkriːt〕鋼筋水泥。forest 〔'fɔːrist〕森林。

〔譯文〕我家在一幢公寓中，我住在高高的大約和森林中最高的一株樹一般高的鋼筋水泥大樓上。

〔解說〕apartment house 係指給水，冷暖氣，電梯等完備的高級住宅。live high up 住的高高的。as tall as～ 與…一般高的 (=as～as)。the tallest 是 tall 的最高級，必須加上 the。

【2】 Our home is so high above the street that we always ride up and down in an elevator.

The elevator is moved from story to story by machinery.

〔單語〕street 〔striːt〕街，道。 elevator 〔'eliveitə〕昇降機 (電梯)。 story 〔'stɔːri〕層樓 (英式為 storey)。 machinery 〔mə'ʃiːnəri〕機械裝置。 is moved 被昇降。 from story to story 一樓一樓地。

〔譯文〕我們家比街道高出太多了，所以常用電梯上、下樓。
電梯係用機器來往於各樓間。

〔解說〕is so high above the street that～ 高出街道如此之多…以致於。so…that「如此…以致於」。up and down 上下。elevator 昇降機。在

美國一般都用 elevator，但在英國則常用 lift 表示。以下數種用語，
在美國與英國也各有不同。

美國	英國	
automobile〔'ɔːtəməbiːl〕car〔kɑː〕	motorcar〔'moutəkɑː〕	汽車
airplane〔'ɛəplein〕, plane〔plein〕	aeroplane〔'ɛərəplein〕	飛機
railroad〔'reilroud〕	railway〔reilwei〕	鐵路
road〔roud〕	way〔wei〕	道路

〖3〗 There are many other families who have their homes in the
building.

Some live on our floor, others live above us and still others
live below us. They also ride up and down in the elevator.

〔單語〕families, family〔'fæmili〕（家庭）的複數。floor〔flɔə〕層、樓。
still〔stil〕還、仍。below〔bilou〕在…之下。

〔譯文〕有好多其他家庭，住在這橦大樓裡。
有些人住在我們同一樓，另有些人住在我們上面，另還有些人住在我們
下面。他們也用電梯上下。

〔解說〕floor 同一層，或同一樓，美國與英國 floor 的表示法不同，二樓美國
為 second floor，英國則為 first floor。There are many other
families who have their homes。在這一句中 who 是關係代名詞，
即 They have their homes…之意。some live~, others live~, and
still others live 即一些住在…，另一些住在…，又另一些住在…。
below as 在我們下方。above us 在我們的上方。

〖4〗 On each floor is a group of rooms called a flat.
One flat has six rooms, all on one floor.
There are a kitchen, a dining-room, a bath-room, bed-rooms,

and a parlour. There is one little room where children play.

〔單語〕group〔gru:p〕群。kitchen〔kitʃin〕廚房。dining-room〔'dainiŋ-rum〕餐廳。bed-room〔'bed-rum〕寢室。parlour〔'pa:lə〕客廳。where〔hwɛə〕表示位置的關係副詞。

〔譯文〕在各層有一組房間卽叫做 flat，每一 flat 有6個房間，都在同一樓。有一個廚房，一個餐廳，一間浴室，幾間臥室和一個客廳，有一個可供小孩遊戲的房間。

〔解說〕a group of room 一組 (一群) 房間。called＝which is called 被稱為。all on one floor 全部在同一層。parlour 客廳，英國又稱為drawing room。one little room where～作…的小房間，where 為關係副詞，請參考文法篇。

【5】The kitchen is the room where meals are cooked. The members of the family sleep in their bedrooms.

Visitors are received in the parlour. We can have a bath in the bath-room.

〔單語〕meal〔mi:l〕餐。cooked〔kukt〕cook (烹飪，煮) 之過去式及過去分詞。visitor〔'vizitə〕訪客。received〔ri'si:vd〕receive (接待) 的過去式及過去分詞。

〔譯文〕廚房是供三餐炊事的房間。家裡的各份子在臥房睡覺。訪客被接待在客廳。我們可在浴室裡洗澡。

〔解說〕the room where～作…的房間 (＝and there)。the members of the family 家庭的分子。are received in 在…被接待。

〔練　習　六〕

用英文寫出下文:

1. 我的家蓋在山丘上。

2. 我叔叔家是二層樓。

   叔叔的房子 uncle's house〔ˈʌŋklz haus〕。是二層樓（蓋成）consist of two stories。

3. 誰住在樓下？

   樓下 downstairs〔ˈdaunˈstɛəz〕。

4. 你睡在樓上嗎？

   樓上 upstairs〔ˈʌpˈstɛəz〕。

2. COPPER (銅)

[6] Copper is a fairly abundant metal. It is second to iron in importance among the metals.

Copper is a soft, extremely ductile and malleable metal with a characteristic reddish-brown color.

〔單語〕 fairly 〔'fɛəli〕 相當的。 abundant 〔ə'bʌndənt〕 豐富的。 metal 〔'metəl〕 金屬。 iron 〔'aiən〕 鐵。 importance 〔im'pɔ:təns〕 重要性。 extremely 〔eks'tri:mli〕 極端的。 ductile 〔'dʌkti(ai)l〕 有靭性的。 malleable 〔'mæliəbl〕 可鍛的。 characteristic 〔kæriktə'ristik〕 特有的，獨特的。 reddish-brown 〔'rediʃ-braun〕 紅棕色的。

〔譯文〕 銅是一種存量相當豐富的金屬，在金屬中，其重要性僅次於鐵。銅是一種軟而極富於展性及可鍛造性的金屬，同時具有一種特殊的紅棕色。

〔解說〕 It is second to iron in importance 它（銅）在重要性次於鐵 (in second to～次於…)。 among (…之間) 用在三者以上。二者之間時用 between。 reddish 帶有紅色的。〔例〕white (白)→whitish. blue (藍)—bluish。

[7] The impure copper is refined electrolytically.

Copper is easily formed into wire, tubes, and sheets. It is an excellent conductor of electricity and is the metal most often used for that

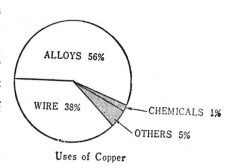

ALLOYS 56%

WIRE 38%

CHEMICALS 1%

OTHERS 5%

Uses of Copper

purpose.

〔單語〕impure〔im'pjuə〕不純的（名詞是 impurity〔im'pju:riti〕不純物）。
refined〔ri'faind〕refine（精鍊）的過去式和過去分詞。
electrolytically〔ilektrou'litikəli〕由電解。wire〔'waiə〕線。
sheet〔ʃi:t〕薄板。excellent〔'eksələnt〕優秀的。

〔譯文〕不純的銅用電解法精鍊。
銅容易加工成線、管、及薄板，它是優良的導電體，而做爲此目的最常
用的金屬。

〔解說〕impure 的相反詞是 pure（純的）。is refined, is formed 被精鍊，被
加工（爲被動式）。electricity（電）的形容詞有 electric 與 electrical,
二者沒有明顯的區分。for that purpose 做爲此目的，that 指導電。

[8] Its principal alloys are brasses, bronzes and coinage metals.
Alloys of copper and zinc are known as brass. Musical instrument,
hardware, and various types of pipes are made from brasses.

〔單語〕principal〔'prinsipəl〕主要的。　　brass〔bræ(ɑ:)s〕黃銅。
bronze〔brɑ(ɔ)nz〕青銅。coinage〔'kɔinidʒ〕鑄幣。zinc〔ziŋk〕鋅。
musical〔'mju:zikəl〕音樂的。hardware〔'hɑ:dwɛə〕金屬器具，五金。
various〔'vɛəriəs〕各種的，不同的。

〔譯文〕其主要的合金有黃銅，青銅及鑄幣金屬。銅與鋅的合金稱爲黃銅。樂器，
五金及各種管子就是黃銅做成的。

〔解說〕are known as 如所知。　musical instrument 樂器。　various types
of 各種形式的。　are made from brasses 由黃銅做成。

[9] Bronze contains copper, tin and zinc.
　　It is used for statues, medals and etc. Aluminum bronze is

used for forgings, bolts and gears.

〔單語〕 contain 〔kən'tein〕 含有。 tin 〔tin〕 錫。 statue 〔'stætjuː〕 雕像。 medal 〔'medəl〕 徽章。 forgings 〔'fɔːdʒiŋgz〕鍛造品。

〔譯文〕 青銅含有銅，錫及鋅。它用於雕像徽章等，鋁青銅用作鍛造物，螺釘及齒輪。

〔解說〕 aluminum bronze 鋁青銅。 is used for 被用作→用作，用於。 gears (＝gear wheels) 齒輪。

〔練 習 七〕

A. 將下文譯成英文:

1. 銅是最有用的金屬之一。

2. 銅應用於很多家庭用的目的。

   應用: apply 〔əp'lai〕

3. 黃銅是銅和鋅的合金。

B. 翻譯下面的英文:

1. Copper is extensively used for guttering, drinking water pipes, and cooking utensils.

   extensively 〔eks'tensivli〕廣泛地。 guttering 〔'gʌtəriŋ〕管道工作。 drinking water pipe 自來水管。 cooking utensil 〔'kukiŋ juː'tensil〕烹飪器具。

2. Its beauty makes it much used for ornamental purposes.

   beauty 〔'bjuːti〕美。 make it much used 使其多用於…。 ornamental 〔ɔːnə'mentəl〕裝飾的。

關於銅的術語研究

銅 (copper) 之拉丁文爲 cuprum，元素記號的 Cu 取自拉丁文，比重8.9融點 (melting point) 1083°C 從硫化鐵礦 pyrites 〔ㇷai'raitiːz〕 首先經過冶金 (metallurgy 〔me'tælədʒi〕) 成爲粗銅 (crude copper)，再電解提鍊變成純銅

（pure copper），是不容易氧化的紅色金屬，熱及電的傳導率 （conductivity）
僅次於銀。在常溫及高溫，均容易加工，作成棒，管，線，板等。多用於電氣零
件，組件，理化學器械等，因合金的成分不同而有各種用途。

3. TANKERS (油輪)

【10】 Oils, gasoline, molasses, and like liquid bulk cargoes are usually transported by means of a type of ship known as a tanker.

〔單語〕 tanker 〔'tæŋkə〕 油輪。 molasses 〔mə'læsiz〕 糖蜜。 bulk 〔bʌlk〕 容積。cargo 〔'kɑ:gou〕 船貨。 transported, transport 〔træns'pɔ:t〕 (輸送) 的過去式, 過去分詞。means 〔mi:nz〕 手法, 手段, 方法。

〔譯文〕 原油, 汽油, 糖蜜及像液體狀的容積大的船貨, 通常用一種叫做油輪的船來運送的。

〔解說〕 molasses 糖蜜, 英國則稱爲 treacle 〔'tri:kl〕, 以複數形使用。 by means of～用…。a type of ship (which is) known as～以～公知的形式的船。

【11】 Most tankers have their machinery located aft and separated from the main tank spaces by means of twin bulkheads forming a narrow empty compartment called a cofferdam.

〔單語〕 located 〔lou'keitid〕 locate (位置) 的過去式, 過去分詞。 aft 〔æ(ɑ:)ft〕 船尾。 separated 〔'sepəreitid〕 separate (分離) 的過去式, 過去分詞。main 〔mein〕 主要。space 〔speis〕 場所, 空間。 twin 〔twin〕 一對的。bulkhead 〔'bʌlkhed〕 隔艙, empty 〔'empti〕 空的。compartment 〔kəm'pɑ:tmənt〕 室。cofferdam 〔'kɔ:fədæm〕 耐油區。

〔譯文〕 大多數油輪的機械設備, 位於船尾, 且用被稱爲耐油區的双層隔艙所形成的狹窄空室與主油艙隔開。

〔解說〕 have located 設置有～ (現在完成式)。 separated from～與…分離。

main tank spaces 主要油貯藏空間，卽爲主油艙。　forming 係說明 twin bulkheads 的現在分詞，a narrow empty compartment called a cofferdam, called 之前，省略了 which is。

[12] Tankers may be divided into three general classes, ocean-going, coastwise, and river craft.

These classes differ very little except in respect to size and service.

〔單語〕ocean-going 〔'ouʃən-'gouiŋ〕遠洋航行。　coastwise 〔'koustwaiz〕近海的，沿岸的。　craft 〔kra:ft〕船舶。　differ 〔difə〕不同。except 〔e'ksept〕除外。respect 〔ris'pekt〕關係、關連。service 〔'sə:vis〕任務。

〔譯文〕油輪可分爲遠洋，近海，及河船三大類。此三類除了有關大小及用途外差別甚微。

〔解說〕may be divided into~ 可被分爲→可分爲。river craft 河船。differ very little 幾乎沒有不同，很少不同。in respect to~ 關於~，在~方面。

[13] Most of the world's modern tankers (about 83 per cent) are propelled by internal combustion engines.

Most American owners, however, still prefer steam propulsion.

〔單語〕propelled 〔prə'peld〕propel (推進) 的過去，及過去分詞。
　　　　internal 〔in'tə:nəl〕內部的。combustion 〔kəm'bʌʃən〕燃燒 (作用)。
　　　　owner 〔'ounə〕所有人。however 〔hau'evə〕但是。
　　　　prefer 〔pri'fə:〕寧願。propulsion 〔prə'pʌlʃən〕推進。

〔譯文〕世界上大部分的現代化油輪 (約83%) 是以內燃引擎來推動。

然而大多數的美國船主寧願使用蒸汽推動方式。

〔解說〕most of 大多數的。the world's modern tankers 世界上現代化的油輪。are propelled 被推動。internal combustion engine 內燃引擎。（在汽缸內爆炸燃燒空氣與燃料使活塞桿往復運動的機械，使用於汽車、飛機、船舶）American Owner 美國的船主。steam propulsion 蒸汽推進。

【14】The steam power plant consumes more fuel than the Diesel, but fuel oil is plentiful and relatively cheap in the United States compared with its abundance and price in foreign countries.

〔單語〕plant〔plæ(ɑ:)nt〕設備，工廠。consume〔kən'sju:m〕消耗。fuel〔'fju:əl〕燃料。plentiful〔'plentiful〕豐富的。relatively〔'relətivli〕比較地。compare〔kəm'pɛə〕比較。foreign〔'fɔ:(ɔ)rin〕外國的。abundance〔ə'bʌndəns〕豐富。

〔譯文〕蒸汽動力設備燃料的消耗較柴油機爲多，但是在美國燃料油比外國豐富而且較便宜。

〔解說〕the steam power plant 蒸汽動力設備。fuel oil 燃油。compared with～ 與…比較。foreign countries 外國。its abundance and price 的 its 指燃油，abundance and price 與前面 plentiful and cheap 重覆，所以翻前句。

【15】The sections through the ship in these sketches show the longitudinal framing that is almost universal in tanker construction, and this system gives great longitudinal strength.

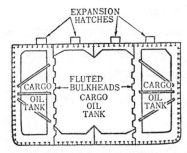

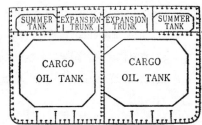

A—Midship section of a ship, a modern
　twin-bulkhead type.

A船體中央斷面圖（現代式二層隔壁式）
　expansion hatches〔iks'pænʃən 'hætʃiz〕
　膨脹艙口蓋。fluted bulkheads 波形隔壁。
　cargo oil tank 貨物油槽。

B—Midship section of a ship, a
　centerlinebulkhead type.

B船體中央斷面圖（中心線隔壁形）
　summer tank 夏季用槽
　expansion tank〔trʌŋk〕膨脹箱

〔單語〕sketch〔sketʃ〕簡圖。 longitudinal〔lɔndʒi'tju:dinəl〕縱向的。
　　　framing〔freimiŋ〕框架，結構。 universal〔ju:ni'və:səl〕一般的，
　　　普通的。construction〔kəns'trʌkʃən〕構造，組立。

〔譯文〕在這些簡圖中的船體斷面， 顯示油輪的構造， 幾乎是普遍使用縱向結
　　　構，這種形式可產生極大的縱向強度。

〔解說〕The sections through the ship 通過船體的斷面圖→船體斷面圖。
　　　longitudinal framing 縱向結構。 is almost universal 幾乎很普遍。
　　　great 極大的。longitudinal strength 縱向強度。

(16) Sketch A shows the modern twin-bulkhead design, and
sketch B the older centerline-bulkhead summer-tank design.

〔單語〕design〔dizain〕設計。

〔譯文〕A圖表示現代化雙層隔艙設計，又B圖是舊式的中心線隔艙夏季油艙設
　　　計。

【解說】 the older 更舊的，舊式的。

〔練 習 八〕

A. 將下文翻譯成英文:

1 油輪是爲了運送油或其他液體所建造的巨大浮槽。

　巨大 huge, enormons 〔i'nɔːməs〕

2 引擎設在船的後部。

　在～後部 at the rear of～

B. 將下文譯爲中文:

1 At the stern is a deckhouse where the members of crew eat and sleep。

　stern 〔stəːn〕船尾。deckhouse 〔'dekhaus〕甲板室。crew 〔kruː〕船員。

2 A tanker is divided into two compartments, as a precaution against fire and to keep the cargo from shifting。

　precaution 〔pri'kɔːʃən〕預防，警戒。to keep～from～…ing 避免…。

　shift 〔ʃift〕移動。

有關船舶種類的術語

after engine boat 〔'æ(ɑː)ftə éndʒin bout〕引擎在船尾的船

boat 〔bout〕小船，小艇

channel steamer 〔'tʃænəlstimə〕海峽連絡船

car ferry 〔kɑː feri〕汽車渡輪

cargo boat 〔'kɑːgou bout〕貨船

coal carrier 〔koul 'kæriə〕煤炭運送船

cold storage boat 〔kould stɔːridʒ bout〕冷藏船

fire boat 〔'faiə bout〕救火船

ice breaker 〔ais 'breikə〕破冰船

launch 〔lɑː(ɔː)ntʃ〕小汽船

life boat 〔laif bout〕救生艇

ocean liner 〔'ouʃən 'lainə〕定期郵輪

oil tanker 〔ɔil 'tæŋkə〕油輪

shallow draft boat 〔'ʃælou dræft bout〕吃水淺的船

sailing vessel 〔'seiliŋ 'vesl〕帆船

sampan 〔'sæmpæn〕舢板

salvage boat 〔'sælveidʒ bout〕救難船

tramp ship 〔træmp ʃip〕
tramper 〔'træmpə〕　　}不定期船

training ship 〔'treiniŋ ʃip〕練習船

tradeship 〔'treidʃip〕商船

trawler 〔'trɔːlə〕撈網船

turbine steamer 〔'təːbin 'stiːmə〕渦輪船

tug (boat) 〔tʌg(bout)〕曳船

merchant ship ['mə:tʃənt ʃip] 商船

whaler ['hweilə] 捕鯨船

motor boat ['moutə bout] 摩托快艇

water boat ['wɔ:tə bout] 給水船

parts of a mixed boat 〔貨客船的各部分〕

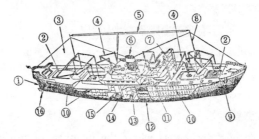

mixed boat 〔mikst bout〕 貨客船

② hatchway ['hætʃwei] 升降口

④ derrick ['derik] 起重機

⑥ funnel 〔fʌnl〕 煙囪

⑧ fore mast 〔fɔə mɑ:(æ)st〕 前桅

⑩ hold 〔hould〕 船倉

⑫ coal bunker 〔koul'bʌŋkə〕 煤庫

⑬ boiler ['bɔilə] 鍋爐

⑮ engine ['endʒin] 引擎

① rudder ['rʌdə] 舵

③ after-mast ['ɑ:ftə mæ(ɑ:)st] 升降口

⑤ antenna 〔æn'tenə〕 天線

⑦ bridge 〔bridʒ〕 船橋

⑨ crew space 〔kru: speis〕 船員室

⑪ cabin passenger ['kæbin 'pæsindʒə]
　　船室, 船客

⑭ bulkhead ['bʌlkhed] 隔壁

⑯ propeller 〔prə'pelə〕 推進器

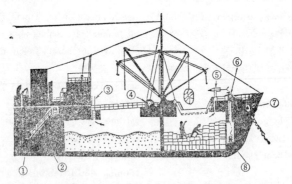

Parts of A cargo carrying skip（貨船的各部名稱）

① machinery space 〔mə'ʃi:nəri speis〕機
　　械室

② accomodation ladder 〔əkɑ(ɔ)mɔ'deiʃən
　　'lædə〕船側梯

③ inlet ventilator 〔inlet ʹventileitə〕 進口通風筒

⑥ windlass 〔ʹwindləs〕 起錨機

⑦ hawsepipe 〔hɔːz paip〕 錨鏈孔

④ winch 〔wintʃ〕 絞盤

⑤ outlet ventilator 〔ʹautlet ʹventileitə〕 出口通風筒

⑧ chain locker〔tʃein ʹlɔkə〕 錨鏈櫃

4. *LATHES* (車床)

[17] The lathe has been called the "king of machine tools", and justly so, because with its many attachments almost any machining operation can be done.

〔單語〕 lathe 〔leið〕車床。　been 〔bi:n〕be 的過去分詞。　machine tool 〔məˈʃi:n tu:l〕工作母機。　justly 〔ˈdʒʌstli〕合適的。　attachment 〔əˈtætʃmənt〕附件。　machining 〔məˈʃi:niŋ〕machine（機械）的現在分詞做機械加工解。　operation 〔ɔpəˈreiʃən〕作業，操作。　done 〔dʌn〕do 之過去分詞。

〔譯文〕 車床一直被稱爲"工作母機之王"，而的確如此，因爲加上它的許多附件幾乎任何機械加工作業，都可完成。

〔解說〕 has been called~ 一直被稱爲……，have (has) been ＋ 過去分詞叫現在完成進行式。表示從過去一直繼續到現在的動作。with its many attachments 用它的很多附件。　machine operation 機械加工作業→機械加工。　machining 是 machine（機械）的形容詞或動詞〔例〕pump 幫浦（名詞）抽水（動詞）。

[18] Size of the lathe is usually based on the maximum size of work that can be machined by a lathe, that is, the diameter and length of the work.

The diameter is specified first, as swing, and length as distance between centers.

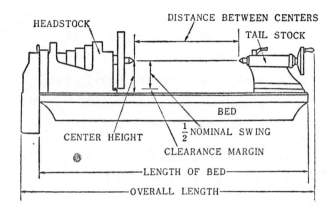

head stock 主軸台。 distance between centers 中心距。 tail stock 尾座。 nominal swing 〔'nɔminəl swiŋ〕公稱攝徑。 bed 床架。 clearance margin 〔'kliərəns 'mɑːdʒin〕邊界間隔。 center height 〔'setə hait〕中心高。 overall 〔'ouvəɔːl〕 length 全長。

〔單語〕 maximum 〔'mæksiməm〕最大的。 specified 〔specifaid〕 specify （指定）的過去式及過去分詞。 swing 〔swiŋ〕擺動。

〔譯文〕 車床尺寸的大小通常是根據可被車床加工的工作物的最大尺寸，卽工作物的直徑及長度。
　　　　直徑首先被指定爲工件擺動時的直徑，而長度爲兩中心針點間的距離。

〔解說〕 is based on～ 根據……，取決於……。　　　that 關係代名詞 can be machined 能被加工（附有 can 的被動式）。　　swing 是圖中 center height （中心高）的 2 倍卽爲可切削的最大尺寸。

[19] The general lathe operations are cylindrical turning, taper turning, boring, facing, and thread cutting.

The engine lathe may be called the all-round lathe. It has automatic feeds, and provided with a lead screw for cutting threads.

〔單語〕cylindrical〔silindrikl〕圓柱形的。　turning〔'tə:niŋ〕圓削。　taper〔'teipə〕推拔，錐度。boring〔'bɔ:riŋ〕搪孔。facing〔'feisiŋ〕面削。thread〔θred〕螺紋。cutting〔kʌtiŋ〕切斷。all-round〔ɔ:l-raund〕萬能的，多方面的。　automatic〔ɔ:tə'mætik〕自動的。　feed〔fi:d〕進刀。　providede provide〔prə'vaid〕(供給，供應)的過去式及過去分詞。lead〔li:d〕引導。

〔譯文〕一般車床之操作爲圓削，推拔，車削，搪孔，平面切削，及螺紋切削。機力車床，可稱之爲萬能車床，它有自動進刀，又備有導螺桿以切削螺紋。

〔解說〕turning 用車床削圓棒→圓削。　face (面削)＋ing (工作動作)＝facing (車面工作)。　　bore (內徑)＋ing＝boring (搪孔工作)engine lathe 機力車床。卽爲普通的車床。is provided with～ 備有……。lead screw 導螺桿 (作螺絲的導桿)。for cutting threads 爲了切削螺紋→切螺紋用。

[20] The turret lathe, vertical lathe, bench lathe, face lathe, automatic lathe and hydraulic lathe are the names of some of the different classes.

In order to learn how to operate any machine, the apprentice must learn the names of the parts and functions of the adjustment and operating handles.

〔單語〕turret〔'tʌrit〕轉塔，六角刀架。　vertical〔'və:tikl〕垂直的，直立的。operate〔'ɔpəreit〕操作。function〔'fʌŋkʃən〕機能，功用。adjustment〔ə'dʒʌstmənt〕調整，調節。

〔譯文〕六角車床，立式車床，枱式車床，平面車床，自動車床，及液壓車床是一些不同種類車床的名稱。

為了學習如何操作，任何機器學徒必須學習了解各部分名稱，調整及操作把手的功用。

〔解說〕turret lathe 六角車床。vertical lathe 立式車床。bench lathe 枱式車床。face lathe 平面車床。automatic lathe 自動車床。hydraulic lathe 液壓車床　the names of some of the different classess 一些不同種類的名稱。in order to～ 為了……。operating handle 操作把手→把手的操作（方法）。

[21] Of course, the best way to get this knowledge is at the lathe itself. In addition to this, the apprentice should bear in mind that considerable information can be obtained by studying the makers' catalogs showing up-to date lathes.

〔單語〕knowledge 〔'nɔlidʒ〕知識。itself 〔it'self〕它本身。bear 〔bɛə〕懷記。mind 〔maind〕心，精神。considerable 〔kən'sidərəbl〕重要的，許多的。information 〔infə'meiʃən〕知識，見聞。obtained 〔əb'teind〕obtain（得到）的過去式及過去分詞。catalog 〔'kætəlɔg〕目錄。(catalogue 英式)。up-to-date 〔'ʌptə'deit〕最近的，最新式的。

〔譯文〕當然，得此知識最好的方法是操作車床本身。再者，學徒應銘記着，研讀廠家所標式的最新式車床的型錄，亦能得到相當多之資料。

〔解說〕of course 當然。the best way to get～ 得到……的最好方法（最上級 best 必須加 the）。is at the lathe itself 就車床其本身→操作車床。in addition to～附加於……此外。should bear in mind that ～ 應留意於……。Showing＝which show 指示，說明。

有關車床的術語研究

車床在工作母機 (machine tools 一機械零件之製造加工機械) 中最常用，所以稱為工作母機之王 (king of machine tools)，是非常重要的加工機械。因其用途，目的不同而有很多種類，以下就其較重要者加以說明。

1. engine lathe（機力車床）一般作業或切螺絲最常用的普通車床，長6～12呎，最先用於切削蒸汽機(steam engine)的汽缸所以至今仍稱為 engine lathe.

2. turret lathe（六角車床）：在六角～八角的台架上裝 6～8 根刀具（cutting tool）者。適用於同形物的多量製造。

3. face lathe（平面車床）：也稱為車面車床，用於直徑大而長度小的機械零件，即為大形物件的車面（facing）和搪孔（boring）用車床。

4. bench lathe（檯式車床）：適合於鐘錶，計器等小型零件精密加工之小形車床。

5. vertical lathe（立式車床）：垂直式搪孔車床，等於將平面車床之主軸直立者。同樣用於切削直徑大長度小的機件內外側。大的直徑2公尺，機械高度達4公尺。

6. hydraulic lathe(液壓車床)：液壓變速車床，利用水壓或油壓轉動車床主軸者。係新式車床，其優點為振動小。

7. automatic lathe（自動車床）：是把六角車床自動化者，適合螺絲，螺絲帽，銷等之大量生產。

8. axle lathe（車軸車床）：用於軸類之切削加工，將軸之兩端用心軸頂針（center）固定從軸的左右同時切削。

9. high-speed lathe（高速車床）：切削速度約為普通車床之四倍。切削能力3～5倍。

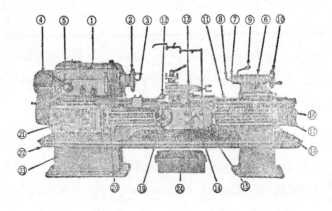

① headstock 車頭　　　　　　　② catch plate 迴轉板
③ live center 活心 (車頭心軸頂針)　④ electric motor 馬達
⑤ change lever for spindle speed 主軸轉速變換手柄
⑥ tail stock 尾架　　　　　　　⑦ tail spindle 尾架伸縮軸
⑧ dead center 死心 (尾架心軸頂針)　⑨ clamping handle 尾架伸縮軸夾緊板
⑩ handle 尾架手輪　　　　　　⑪ bed 車床身
⑫ carriage 拖板　　　　　　　⑬ compound rest 複式刀架
⑭ apron 前覆部　　　　　　　⑮ half-nut lever 半螺帽開關手柄
⑯ lead (ing) screw 導螺桿　　　⑰ feed rod 進給傳動桿
⑱ auxiliary lever and rod 開動停車輔助操作桿
⑲ handle for longitudinal feed 縱間移動手輪
⑳ starting lever 起動手柄　　　㉑ feed change gear box 進給變換齒輪箱
㉒ oil receiver 油盤　　　　　　㉓ legs 車脚
㉔ oil reservoir 盛油盤

有關工作母機的術語研究

　　工作母機 (machine tool) 的定義是「用於製造一般機械器具的機械」其目的在於改變金屬材料的形狀或精密加工其表面。以下就其常用者加以說明。

1. lathe (車床): 已在「有關車床的術語研究」中詳細說明。

2. milling machine (銑床): 為次於車床的重要切削加工機械。乃利用裝於軸上的圓形刀具 (銑刀)，切製齒輪，螺絲等複雜工件。

3. planing machine (龍門刨床): 又稱為 planer 即為平削機，用於削平長而大的平面。

4. shaping machine (牛頭刨床): 又稱為 shaper 即為形削機，用於小形工件的平面切削，切溝。

5. slotting machine (插床) 又稱為 slotter 即為縱削機，刀具上下，移動往下時可切削工件的垂直面，又可切削圓弧形及鍵溝。

6. drilling machine (鑽床) 裝上鑽頭 (drill) 在工件上開孔的機械。

7. boring machine (搪床) 用於切削圓筒物件之內側。有豎立形及橫臥形。

8. grinding machine (磨床) 又稱為 grinder 即為研磨機用以作為上述機械切削後之最後精密加工。

5. *WHAT IS AUTOMATION?* (何為自動化)

〔22〕 Automation is a new American technical term. But the source of this word itself is not clear. Perhaps it means automatic operation of a machine or of a number of machines.

〔單語〕 automation 〔ɔ:tə′meiʃən〕 自動化，自動操作。 technical 〔′teknikəl〕 工業的。 term 〔tə:m〕 術語。 source 〔sɔ:s〕 來源。

〔譯文〕 自動化是一個新的美國工業術語，但此語本身的來歷並不清楚。可能它是表示一部或一些機器的自動操作。

〔解說〕 American technical term 美國的工業術語。 this word itself 這個字語本身。 is not clear 不清楚。 mean 意味，表示。 automatic opperation 自動操作。 of a number of machines 一些機器。

〔23〕 Some American engineers say that automation is confined to transfer machines and electronics.

　　Others regard automation as meaning simply the mechanization of work processes.

〔單語〕 confine 〔kən′fain〕 限於，局限於。　　　transfer 〔træns′fə:〕 傳送。 electronics 〔ilek′trɔniks〕 電子工學。　　　regard 〔ri′gɑ:d〕 視爲。 meaning 〔′mi:niŋ〕 意味。 mechanization 〔mekənai′zeiʃən〕 機械化。 process 〔′prouses〕 過程，方法。

〔譯文〕 一些美國工程師們主張自動化是僅限於傳送機械和電子設備方面。其他人認爲自動化一詞，僅是將工作過程機械化的意思。

〔解說〕 say that 主張，說。　 is confined to: 被限於。　 transfer machine 傳送機械（參考自動操作有關術語）。　 regard~as meaning 認爲…意

義。work process 工作過程。

【24】 So we must rethink, redesign and reform about our machines and apparatuses.

Recently we can find the word "automation" in some dictionaries, but the exact meaning suitable for this new term is not explained clearly.

〔單語〕 rethink 〔riːθiŋk〕 再思考。redesign 〔ˈriːdizain〕 再設計。
reform 〔riːˈfɔːm〕 改造。apparatus 〔æpəˈreitəs〕 器具，裝置。
recently 〔ˈriːsntli〕 近來。clearly 〔ˈkliəli〕 清楚地。

〔譯文〕 所以我們必需重新思慮與設計，以改造我們的機械及器具。近來我們可以在某些字典中找到"自動化"這個字眼，但是適和於這個新術語的正確含義仍未被解釋清楚。

〔解說〕 re～代表「再」的接頭語，re＋think（想）＝rethink 再想，再考慮。suitable for～適於…。is not explained: 沒有被解釋（否定的被動態）。

【25】 Generally speaking, a factory or a works equipped with automation system can greatly reduce working hours and operate with relatively few workers.

Automation is also applied to the loading, transportation and unloading of all kinds of goods.

〔單語〕 equip 〔iˈkwip〕 裝置。greatly 〔ˈgreitli〕 大大地。reduce 〔riˈdjuːs〕 減少。 loading 〔ˈloudiŋ〕 載貨。 unloading 〔ʌnˈloudiŋ〕 卸下。transportation 〔trænspɔːˈteiʃən〕 運輸。

〔譯文〕 一般來說，一個裝置自動化系統的製造廠或工廠，能够大大地減少工作時間，並以較少數之工人操作。

自動化也被應用在裝載，運輸及卸下所有種類的貨品。

〔解說〕generally speaking 一般而言。　　equipped with～裝置～設備～。
automation system 自動化系統。　　　working hours 工作時間。
is applied to～之用於… loading 裝貨（動名詞）。　unloading 卸貨
（動名詞）all kinds of～ 所有種類的。

〔練　習　九〕

翻譯下列英文:

1. When was automation introduced in the American automobile industry?
   introduce〔intrə'dju:s〕. 介紹。

2. The principle of automation is not new. One of its earliest applications
   began about 175 years ago in the operation of a continuous flour mill.
   principle〔pri'nsipl〕原理，原則。continuous〔kən'tinjuəs〕連續的。flour mill
   〔flauəmil〕製粉機。

3. To design an automatic control system is not always as easy as it
   may seem.
   automatic control system 自動控制方式。is not always 不一定是。

自動操作有關的術語

1　自動操作: automation 是 automatic（自動的）與 operation（操作）合
   起來，而成的美國語，指代替人類動作，調整，控制的機械裝置。應用電子
   工學中的溫度計，光度計 photometer〔foutə'mitə〕壓力計 pressure gauge
   〔'preʃə geidʒ〕流量計 flow meter〔flou'mitə〕 等，使機械裝置自動化，
   以達到節省人工，動作確實之目的。

2　傳送機械 transfer machine: 這也是新的名詞，而尚未有確定譯語。工作
   物加工時，將加工所使用的自動機械，依照加工順序加以排列，機械與機械
   之間，加上自動輸送設備之一群裝置，應用這種裝置能將許多工作物同時加

工。工作物之裝上，加工，卸下，以至移至下一步的加工皆能自動進行。尚且在加工中能將工作物之形狀尺寸自動量度，如有異樣，機器能自動停止。

3 電子學 electronics: 也稱電子技術，電子工業。電子管（眞空管）等之迴路有關的科學，以及應用技術。此外像電晶體 transister 〔træn′zistə〕，鍺 Ge germanium 〔dʒəːˈmeinjəm〕二積體 diode 〔ˈdaioud〕等的半導體，電子裝置及其迴路也被包含在內。在應用方面如通信，天文，火箭 rocket 〔ˈrɔkit〕，雷達 radar 〔ˈreidə〕計算機，醫療等，範圍廣泛。

6. *THE ORIGIN OF THE STEAM TURBINE*
(蒸汽機之起源)

[26] One day in 1897, when the British were baving a Naval Review at Spithead, a strange little craft came to close to the warships. A speedy destroyer was sent out to question it.

〔單語〕 origin 〔ʹɔridʒin〕 起源，起始。 steam turbine 〔stiːm ʹtəːbin〕 蒸汽輪機。 Naval Review 〔ʹneivəl riʹvjuː〕 閱艦式 Spithead 〔spithed〕 地名。close 〔klouz〕 接近，迫近。 warship 〔ʹwɔːʃip〕 軍艦。speedy 〔ʹspiːdi〕 快速的。destroyer 〔disʹtrɔiə〕 驅逐艦。

〔譯文〕 1897年某日，在 Spithead 英軍舉行閱艦式時，一隻陌生的小艇駛近軍艦。一隻快速的驅逐艦被派遣去查詢。

〔解說〕 One day 有一天。 the British 英軍。 1897是年代，讀成 eighteen-ninety seven。were having 舉行爲過去進行式。come to close to~ 迫近來。 was sent out. 被派遣，被送出 (sent out 送出)。
to question 詢問 (question 有名詞與動詞兩種用法，在這裡是動詞「詢問」「質問」之意)。

[27] But an amazing thing happened. The little mystery ship suddenly increased speed and flashed away at the high speed of 34 1/2 knots.
　　The destroyer, the fastest ship in the fleet, was left far behind.

〔單語〕 amazing 〔əʹmeiziŋ〕 可驚的，吃驚的。 happen 〔ʹhæpn〕 (事故，變故) 發生，偶然發生。mystery 〔ʹmistəri〕 不可思議，神秘。suddenly 〔ʹsʌdnli〕 突然地，忽然地。 increase 〔inʹkriːs〕 增加。 flash 〔flæʃ〕

（閃光般在眼前）掃過。　knot〔nɑ(ɔ)t〕浬，船泊行進速度之單位，俗稱海里（nautical mile）。　1 海里＝1853米。　fleet〔fi:t〕艦隊。left leave〔li:v〕（遺留）之過去式，過去分詞 behind〔bi'haind〕在後的，後方的。

〔譯文〕但是一個可驚的事發生，這小的神秘船突然增速而以每小時34½浬之閃電似的速度離去，這艦隊中最快速的驅逐艦遠被拋在後面。

〔解說〕an amazing thing happened 一個可驚的事突然發生。　flashed away 閃光似的離去。at the high speed of～ 以…的高速。34½ 讀成 thirty four and a (one) half。The destroyer, the fastest ship in the fleet 這艦隊中最快速船的驅逐艦（這種場合，the fastest ship in the fleet 是說明 The destroyer 的詞句，二者同格稱爲同格名詞）。was left 被遺留。far behind 遠在後方。

[28] The little ship turned out to be Sir Charles Parsons' turbinia, which had a new type of steam engine invented by Parsons.

He called the engine a turbine. It did not have pistons.

〔單語〕Sir〔sə:〕卿（在英國騎士爵 knight〔nait〕與準男爵〔bærənit〕人名所冠的稱號。　Sir Charles Parsons' turbinia〔sə:tʃɑ:lz 'pɑ:snz 'tə:binjə〕查爾斯帕森卿的渦輪。　invent〔in'vent〕發明。　piston〔'pistən〕活塞。

〔譯文〕這小艇顯示爲查爾斯帕森卿的渦輪號，那是帕森氏發明的新型蒸汽引擎。他稱這引擎爲渦輪。它沒有活塞。

〔解說〕turned out to be～ 顯示結果是，（turn out 想像是…結果却是）。Sir 是對國家有功勞者所授與的爵位在科學方面 Sir Isaac Newton 伊薩克，牛頓爵士（物理學家、數學家，萬有引力、微積分之發明者）。

Sir Henry Bessemer 亨利貝思默（貝思默轉爐之發明者）。

關係代名詞 which 之前若有「，」則其後通常不譯作「然而」
而當 and it （乃是）（關係代名詞之連續用法，參照工業英文法關係代
名詞）。a New type of～ 新形式之。invented by～由某人之發明
(invented 之前應補以 which was).

【29】 A strong jet of steam blew against hundreds of small fan
blades, forcing them to turn a shaft around and around within a
strong steel casing.

The new engine had power and speed, and did not need much
steam.

〔單語〕 jet 〔dʒet〕 噴射。blew 〔bluː〕 blow（吹）的過去式。fan blade 〔fæn
bleid〕 扇頁。forcing force（强制）的現在分詞。within 〔wiðin〕 在
…之內。casing 〔ˈkeisiŋ〕 套蓋。need 〔niːd〕 需要。

〔譯文〕 强力蒸汽噴向數百的小扇頁， 迫使它們在堅固鋼套內連續旋轉。
這新引擎具有動力及速度，而不需要多量的蒸氣。

〔解說〕 a strong jet of steam 强力蒸氣的噴射。　　blew against～吹向…。
hundreds of 數百的。forcing them to turn＝and forced them to
turn 迫使它們旋轉。　around and around 繼續轉動。　power and
speed 動力及速度。much steam 多量蒸氣。

【30】 The small size of the engine was important, too.

In the first steamship, the clumsy engines took up more than
a third of the inside space.

These old-fashioned engines used so much coal that there
was not much room left for cargo.

〔單語〕steamship〔'sti:mʃip〕汽船。　clumsy〔'klʌmzi〕笨拙的，不雅觀的。
old-fashioned〔ould-'fæʃənd〕舊式的，老式的。

〔譯文〕引擎的小型化是很重要的。最初的汽船，其笨拙的引擎佔內部空間的$\frac{1}{3}$
以上。那些舊式的引擎須用太多的煤炭而無多餘空間存放貨物。

〔解說〕The small size of the engine 小型的引擎。　took up 佔據。
more than~ 多於~。a third $\frac{1}{3}$。　inside space 內部空間。
used so much coal that 須用太多的煤炭而使… (so that 太…而
使…，為相關連接詞)。there was not room left for cargo 沒有多
餘空間存放貨物 (room 並非室而是空間)。

[31] For many years men had been working to make steam
engines smaller and cheaper to operate.

Parsons' turbine proved to be the best and most economical
steam engine ever built.

Turbine-type engines are used by most of the great passenger
liners and warships today.

〔單語〕prove〔pru:v〕證明。economical〔i:kə'nɑ(ɔ)mikəl〕經濟的。
turbine-type engine 渦輪引擎。passenger liner〔'pæsindʒə 'lainə〕
定期客輪。

〔譯文〕多年來人們從事製造更小，更便宜的引擎來操作。帕森式渦輪被證明為
迄今所製中最佳最經濟的蒸汽引擎。今日渦輪式的引擎被大多數大型定
期客輪及軍艦所使用。

〔解說〕had been working to make 一直從事 (研究) 製造 (進行式過去完
成式此形是「had been＋現在分詞」請參考工業用英文法「時態」)。
smaller and cheaper 更小型更便宜。to operate 來操作 (不定詞)。

proved to be～證明爲…。the best and most economical 最佳及最經濟的。ever built 曾經建造中的。most of 大多數。

【32】Recently, a new type of turbines called the gas turbine is widely used instead of steam turbines.

It is far more effective and speedy than any other steam turbine.

〔單語〕gas turbine 〔gæs ′təːbin〕氣體渦輪。

〔譯文〕最近，新型的渦輪稱爲氣體渦輪廣被使用以取代蒸汽渦輪。它是遠較任何其他蒸汽渦輪有效及快速。

〔解說〕is widely used 廣被使用。instead of～取代～。far more effective 遠較有效。

有關渦輪術語之研究

turbine 渦輪: 使流體接觸扇葉，其運動的能量 kinetic energy 〔kai′netik ′enədʒi〕可把回轉運動變爲動力成回轉式原動機。可區分爲水渦輪，蒸汽渦輪，氣體渦輪，使用於發電、船舶等。

1. water turbine 水渦輪: 將水所帶有之能量，速度及壓力作用於渦輪之葉片上，使轉換爲機械能。因效率高。故廣用在水力發電廠之原動機上。

2. steam turbine 蒸氣渦輪: 由鍋爐所產生之高壓蒸氣經由噴嘴 (nozzle) 噴出而成爲高速蒸氣噴流以轉動渦輪之葉片以得動力之熱機 (heat engine)。

3. gas turbine 氣體渦輪: 將高溫高壓之燃燒氣體經膨脹後以帶動渦輪葉片之廻轉式內燃機。

有關船用引擎術語

after engine 〔′ɑːftə ′endʒin〕後部引擎　　　auxiliary engine 〔ɔː′gziljəli ′endʒin〕補
boat hoisting engine 〔bout ′hɔistiŋ　　助引擎

'endʒin〕揚艇機
Diesel engine 〔'diːzəl 'endʒin〕柴油引擎
donkey engine 〔'dɑ(ɔ)ki 'endʒin〕補機
double expansion engine〔'dʌbl eks'pænʃən 'endʒin〕二段膨脹引擎
fan 〔fæn〕engine 送風式引擎
main 〔mein〕engine 主機
internal combustion engine 內燃引擎
triple expansion engine 〔'tripl eks'pænʃən 'endʒin〕三段式膨脹引擎

compound engine 〔kəm'pəund 'endʒin〕二段膨脹引擎
double acting engine〔'dʌbl æktiŋ 'endʒin〕復動引擎
dynamo 〔dainəmou〕engine 電動引擎
hot-bulb 〔hɔt bʌlb〕engine 熱頭式引擎
marin 〔məriːn〕engine 船用引擎
petroleum 〔pe'troljən〕engine 石油引擎
steam 〔stiːm〕engine 蒸汽引擎

有關鍋爐術語

auxiliary boiler 〔ɔːg'ziljəli 'bɔilə〕補助鍋爐
donkey boiler 〔dɑ(ɔ)nki 'bɔilə〕補助鍋爐
exhaust boiler 〔eg'zɔːst 'bɔilə〕排氣鍋爐
main boiler 〔mein 'bɔilə〕主鍋爐
marine boiler 〔mə'riːn 'bɔilə〕船用鍋爐
Scotch boiler 〔skɑ(ɔ)tʃ 'bɔilə〕蘇格蘭鍋爐
steam boiler 〔stiːm 'bɔilə〕蒸氣鍋爐
tubular boiler 〔'tjuːbjulə 'bɔilə〕煙管鍋爐
water tube boiler 〔'wɔːtə tjuːb' bɔilə〕水管鍋爐

7. *ELEMENTS AND SYMBOLS* (元素與符號)

[33] Elements are the basic constituents of all matter. An element is the simplest form of matter.

　It cannot be formed from simpler substances, nor can it be decomposed into simpler varieties of matter.

〔單語〕element 〔'elimənt〕（化學）元素。 symbol 〔'simbəl〕符號，記號。 constituent 〔kəns'titjuənt〕構成要素成份。 matter 〔'mætə〕物質。 nor 〔nɔ:〕…也不。 decompose 〔di:kəm'pouz〕分解。 varieties, variety 〔və'raiəti〕多種多樣之複數。

〔譯文〕元素是一切物質的基本構成要素，元素是最簡單形的物質，它不能由更簡單的物質所形成，也不能分解爲各種不同的物質。

〔說解〕basic constituent 基本的構成要素。of all matter 一切物質中的。 the simplest form of～ 最簡單形狀的～。it cannot be formed～, nor can it be decomposed 它不能被形成…，也不能被分解……。 varieties of matter 種種的物質。

[34] Iron, gold, carbon and nitrogen are elements, but sugar is not——it can be broken down into oxygen, hydrogen and carbon. There are in fact over 90 elements. All matter is made up out of these elements.

〔單語〕carbon 〔'ka:bən〕碳。 nitrogen 〔'naitrədʒən〕氮。 sugar 〔'ʃugə〕砂糖。 oxygen 〔'a(ɔ)ksidʒən〕氧。 hydrogen 〔haidridʒən〕氫。 fact 〔fækt〕事實，實際。

〔譯文〕鐵，金，碳，以及氮是元素，但是糖並不是一糖能被分解成爲氧，氫，和碳。實際上有90種以上的元素。一切物質由這些元素造成。

〔解說〕can be broken down into 能被分解爲…… (break up 分解，分析)。

is made up out of 以……作成 (out of～從)

[35] The next table is a list of the more commonly known elements together with their chemical symbols.

Element	Symbol	Element	Symbol
Aluminum	Al	Carbon	C
Arsenic	As	Chlorin (e)	Cl
Bromine	Br	Copper	Cu
Calcium	Ca	Gold	Au
Helium	He	Platinum	Pt
Hydrogen	H	Plutonium	Pu
Iron	Fe	Radium	Ra
Lead	Pb	Silicon	Si
Mercury	Hg	Silver	Ag
Neon	Ne	Sodium	Na
Nickel	Ni	Sulfur	S
Nitrogen	N	Tin	Sn
Oxygen	O	Uranium	U
Phosphorus	P	Zinc	Zn

〔單語〕list 〔list〕表，一覽表。　　Arsenic 〔'ɑːsənik〕鉮。　　Chlorin (e) 〔'klɔːrin〕氯。Bromine 〔'broumin〕溴　Calcium 〔'kælsiəm〕鈣 。 Helium 〔'hiːljəm〕氦。　plutonium 〔pluː'touniəm〕鈈。　Radium 〔'reidiəm〕鐳。Silicon 〔silikən〕矽。Silver 〔'silvə〕銀。　Neon 〔'niːən〕氖。Sodium 〔'soudiəm〕鈉。Nickel 〔'nikl〕鎳。Sulfur 〔'sʌlfə〕硫。Tin 〔tin〕錫。Uranium 〔juː'reniəm〕鈾。Phosphorus 〔'fɔsfərəs〕磷。

〔譯文〕下表是最常用的化學元素附以化學符號的一覽表。(以下翻譯省略)

〔解說〕more commonly known elements 最普通熟知之元素。known 是 know 之過去分詞，在此被用爲形容詞。together with～ 一起。

[36] As already stated there are over 90 elements at present, but Nuclear Scientists believe that this number may possibly grow at least to 104 in the near future.

〔單語〕Nuclear ['nju:kliə] 原子核的，原子力的。scientist ['saiəntist] 科學家。 believe [bi'li:v] 相信，認爲。possibly ['pɔsəbli] 大概，恐怕 (=perhaps)。future ['fju:tʃə] 將來。

〔譯文〕如所敍述的，目前有90多個元素，但核子科學家相信在不久將來這個數目很可能增加到至少104個。

〔解說〕As already stated 敍述的。at present 目前，現在。nuclear scientist 原子科學家。 believe that～ 相信是……(that 是連接詞)。 may possibly grow to～ 可能發展到～。at least 至少。in the near future 不久的將來。

[37] Generally speaking, the symbols are made up of the principal letter or letters in the name of the element.

　　The symbols of elements known in antiquity are taken from their Latin names: Copper (Cuprum) Cu; Gold (Aurum) Au; Iron (Ferrum) Fe; Lead (Plumbum) Pb; Mercury (Hydrargyrum) Hg; Silver (Argentum) Ag; Tin (Stannum) Sn, etc.

〔單語〕principal ['prinsipəl] 第1(位) 的 antiquity [ænti'kwiti] 古代，太古。Latin ['lætin] 拉丁 (文)。

〔譯文〕一般而言，這些符號是以元素名稱之第一字母或兩字母所組成。

古代所知元素之符號是得自其拉丁名字，如銅 Cu 是 Cuprum，金
Au 是 Aurum，鐵 Fe 是 Ferrum，鉛 Pb 是 Plumbum，水銀 Hg
是 Hydrargyrum，銀 Ag 是 Aregentum，錫 Sn 是Stannum 等。

〔解說〕generally speaking 一般而言（用動名詞之習慣語）。 are made up
of～ 從……而成。principal letter or letters 第一位的字母或其他
字母。known in antiquity 在古代就知道的（＝that is known…）。
are taken from 被取之於。Latin name 拉丁名詞。

【38】These symbols are very important in chemistry for they
represent three things:

1. The name of an element.

2. One atom of an element.

3. A quantity of the element equals in weight to its atomic
weight.

〔單語〕chemistry 〔'kemistri〕化學。 represent 〔repri'zent〕表示，意味着。
atom 〔'ætɔm〕原子。 quantity 〔'kwɑ(ɔ)ntiti〕量，數量。 atomic
weight 〔ə'tɑ(ɔ)mik weit〕原子量。

〔譯文〕這些符號在化學上是十分重要的，因爲這些符號代表着三種事項
1.元素之名稱，2.元素之一原子，3.元素的量與它原子量的重量相同。

〔解說〕for 是連接詞，意思比 because 輕。three things 三個事項。equals
in weight to～ 重量與……相同。

【39】For example, when we write the symbol O, we mean not
only the name oxygen, but we also represent a single oxygen
atom with this symbol.

What is perhaps most important of all, since oxygen has an atomic weight of 16, the symbol O stand for 16 units of weight of this element.

〔單語〕single 〔siŋgl〕單一（的）

〔譯文〕例如，當我們寫符號O，我們不僅指氧氣之名稱，而且也用此符號代表一單原子的氧氣。

或許所有之中最重要的是因氧有16的原子量，此符號O卽代表此元素之重量爲16單位。

〔解說〕for example 例如。 not only～, but also～ 不僅……而且……。mean 意味着。single oxygen atom 單一氧原子。with this symbol 以這個符號。what is most important 最重要的事是（what 是無前置詞之特別關係代名詞）。

[40] This may be 16 grams, or 16 pounds, or 16 tons. We can select any system of weight units we need when we use symbols to indicate quantities of elements.

〔單語〕select 〔si′lekt〕選擇。indicate 〔′indikeit〕指示。

〔譯文〕這可以是16克，或16磅，或16噸。當我們用這些符號去表示元素之量時我們可以選擇任何我們需要的重量單位系統。

〔解說〕may be 可以是，可能是。any system of weight units 任何重量單位系統。we need (= that we need) 我們需要的。

〔練 習 十〕

翻譯下列英文:

1. An atom is the smallest particle of an element capable of showing

the properties of the element.

particle〔′pɑ:tikl〕分子，微分子，粒子。 capable of〔′keipəbl ɔv〕能…。 properties〔′prɑ(ɔ)pətis〕 property（特性）的複數。

2. Atomic number of an atom is the sum of the electrons in the shells surrounding the atom.

atomic number 原子序數。 electron〔i′lektrɔn〕電子。 shell〔ʃel〕（構成原子之電子的）殼。 surround〔sə′raund〕圍繞。

3. the atomic weight of an atom is the sum of the number of protons and neutrons in the nucleus.

proton〔′proutɔn〕質子。 neutron〔′nju:trɔn〕中子。 nucleus〔′niu:kliəs〕原子核。

4. Symbols stand for the name of an element, one atom of the element, and one atomic weight's worth of the element.

one atomic weight's worth 一原子量之值

化學術語之研究

catalyst〔′kætəlist〕觸媒

catalyzer〔′kætəlaizə〕觸媒

chemical action〔′kemikəl ′ækʃən〕化學作用

chemical formula〔′kemikəl ′fɔ:mjulə〕化學式

chemical industry〔′kemikəl ′indəstri〕化學工業

chemical reaction〔′kemikəl ri′ækʃən〕化學反應

chemical change〔′kemikəl tʃeindʒ〕化學變化

extraction〔eks′trækʃən〕抽出

mixture〔′mikstʃə〕混合物

chemist〔′kemist〕化學家

chemistry〔′kemistri〕化學

composition〔kɑ(ɔ)mpə′ziʃən〕組成

compound〔kəm′paund〕化合（物）

decomposition〔dikɑmpə′ziʃən〕分解

distillation〔disti′leiʃən〕蒸餾（作用）

distilled water〔distild ′wɔ:tə〕蒸餾水

natural gas〔′nætʃurəl gæs〕天然氣

oil gas〔ɔil gæs〕石油氣

primary air〔′praiməri ɛə〕一次空氣

secondary air〔′sekəndəri ɛə〕二次空氣

solvent〔′sɔlvənt〕溶劑溶媒

weathering〔′weðəriŋ〕風化（作用）

8. *A NUCLEAR POWER PLANT* (核子發電廠)

[41] The main parts of a nuclear power plant are fuel, the moderator, and the coolant.

The fuel is a radioactive metal, such as uranium, plutonium, or thorium.

〔單語〕moderator〔'mɔdəreitə〕減速劑（原子爐中之中子之石墨，重氫等）。 coolant〔'ku:lənt〕冷却劑。radioactive〔'rediou'æktiv〕放射性的，有放射性的。thorium〔'θɔ:riəm〕釷（符號＝Th）

〔譯文〕核子發電廠之主要部分是燃料，減速劑，及冷却劑。 燃料是放射性金屬 例如：鈾、釙、或釷。

〔解說〕nuclear power plant 核子發電廠（＝atomic power plant），power plant（＝power station）發電廠。main parts：主要部分。such as: 例如，像…。

[42] Usually it is made into rods, about the size of baseball bats, which are pushed through a framework by machinery. At least one plant, however, will have its fuel in the form of a liquid-uranium salt dissolved in water.

〔單語〕rod〔rɔd〕棒。push〔puʃ〕推送。framework〔'freimwə:k〕構架。 dissolve〔di'zɔlv〕溶解。

〔譯文〕通常燃料是作成約像棒球棒大小之棒，此棒被機械推送進入構架。但，] 至少有一發電廠，其燃料是以溶解在水中之液狀鈾鹽之形狀的。

〔解說〕about the size of baseball bats 約棒球棒大小。which＝and it 作

為連結前句用。　are pushed through～被推送進入。　at least 至少。
in the form of～以……之形狀。　　liquid-uranium salt 液狀鈾鹽。
dissolved in water 被溶於水 (dissolved 之前省略 which is)。

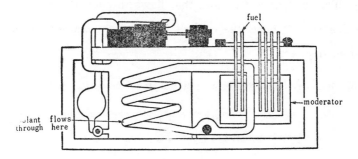

〔圖之說明〕核子反應爐的各部分。　此反應爐用水作爲冷却劑。其他的可用氣體，例如二氧
化碳，或熔解金屬，如液體鈉。
reactor 〔ri:′æktə〕反應爐。carbon dioxide 〔′ka:bən dai′ɔksaid〕二氧化碳。

【43】 The moderator is the stuff of which the framework holding
the fuel is made, usually graphite.

The purpose of moderator is to slow down the neutrons that fly
out from the explosion of each atom, so that they shall penetrate
other atoms and make them explode, also.

〔單語〕stuff 〔stʌf〕材料，原料。　　graphite 〔′græfait〕石墨，黑鉛。
explosion 〔iksp′louʒən〕爆發。　　penetrate 〔′penitreit〕穿透。
explode 〔iks′ploud〕爆發。

〔譯文〕減速劑是做爲構成支撑燃料的材料，通常是石墨。
減速劑的目的是減慢從各原子爆發飛出來之中子，因此它們也能穿透另
外原子而使其爆炸。

〔解說〕the stuff of which the fremework holding the fuel 構架支撑燃料
之材料。　the neutrons that fly out from 從……飛出來之中子。

so that 因此。make explode～使其爆炸。

【44】 Neutrons that go **too fast** simply bounce off the neighboring atom. The coolant is the fluid that flows through the reactor.

　　The reactor heats the **coolant** up to a temperature of several hundred degrees.

〔單語〕bounce 〔bauns〕跳起來。neighboring 〔'neibərin〕鄰近的。

〔譯文〕中子的運動過快只使鄰近原子跳出。冷却劑是流通於反應爐之液體。
　　　　反應爐之熱使冷却劑溫度上升到好幾百度。

〔解說〕neutrons that go too fast 中子運動過快。bounce off 跳出。
　　　　neighboring atom 鄰近原子。　the fluid that flows through the
　　　　reactor 流經反應爐之液體。heats～up to～熱到～。several hundred
　　　　degrees 好幾百度。

【45】 Then the coolant is pumped out of the **reactor** and through a kind of radiator called a heat exchanger.

　　Here it boils water, and is itself cooled down.

　　The coolant may be water, a gas, or a molten metal.

〔單語〕radiator 〔'reidieitə〕冷却器，放熱器。　　heat exchanger
　　　　〔hi:t iks'tʃeindʒə〕熱交換器。

〔譯文〕然後，冷却劑從反應爐抽出且通過一種叫熱交換器之散熱器。
　　　　在此煮沸水，而它本身被冷却下來。
　　　　冷却劑可能是水，氣體或是一種熔融金屬。

〔解說〕is pump out of 被泵抽出（此處 pump 是當動詞用，用泵抽出之意）。
　　　　is itself cooled down 其本身被冷却下來→自然冷却。may be 可能
　　　　是。molten metal 熔融金屬（molten 是 melt 之過去分詞，在此當形

容詞用）。

【46】 The molten metal that is now being tried out is sodium.

The steam produced by the heat **exchanger** flows through **a** turbine, and the turbine in turn runs an electric generator.

〔單語〕 produce 〔prə'dju:s〕 發生，製造。　electric generator 〔i'lektrik 'dʒenəreitə〕 發電機。

〔譯文〕 現在被試驗出的熔融金屬是鈉。

由熱交換器製造出之蒸氣通過渦輪，而由渦輪連續帶動發電機。

〔解說〕 the molten metal 熔融金屬。下面之 that 是關係代名詞。 is now being tried out 目前被試驗着（被動式之現在進行式）。try out 試驗出。 flow through 流通過……。 in turn 次第，連續。 electric generator 發電機，亦可單用 generator。

【47】 Many nuclear power plants are already generating electric current in the United States, England, and Soviet Union.

Engineers are also drawing up designs for nuclear-powered locomotives and airplanes.

〔單語〕 Soviet Union 〔'souviet 'ju:njən〕 蘇聯。 locomotive 〔'loukəmoutiv〕 火車頭。

〔譯文〕 在美國，英國及蘇聯已經有許多核子發電廠，發出電流。

工程師們也正在繪製核子動力火車頭及飛機之設計圖。

〔解說〕 are already generating 已經產生之中。 are drawing up designs 繪製設計圖。powered 作爲動力。

〔練 習 十一〕

翻譯下列英文:

1. Engineers are now experimenting with a new kind of steam engine, which gets its heat, not from coal or from fuel oil, but from a machine called a nuclear reactor.

   experimenting experiment 作實驗之現在分詞。

2. About sixty years ago, scientists learned that an atom is not a simple lump, but a complicated little group composed of smaller particles whirling about one another, somewhat as planet revolve about the sun.

   lump〔'lʌmp〕團, 塊。complicate〔'kɔmplikeit〕複雜的。composed〔kəm'pouzd〕of…由……構成。whirl〔hwəːl〕繞……轉。

   somewhat〔'sʌmhwɔt〕稍稍。planet〔'plænit〕行星。revolve〔rivɔlv〕旋轉。

有關原子能之術語

① nuclear reactor, nucleal reactor, atomic reactor 核子反應爐, 核反應爐, 原子爐
   nuclear energy 核能
   nuclear fission〔'fiʃən〕原子分裂
   nuclear fuel 原子核燃料
   nuclear physics 核子物理
   nuclear power plant 核子發電廠
   nucleonics〔njuː'kliɔniks〕核工學, 核子物理學
   nucleus 核子

② atom 原子
   atomic, atomical 原子的
   atomic energy 原子能
   atomic fission 原子分裂
   atomic hypothesis〔hai'pɔθisis〕原子論
   atomic number 原子序
   atomic pile 原子爐
   atomic ship 原子船
   atomic theory 原子理論
   atomic value 原子價
   atomics 原子學

研　究　編

1. SAFETY PRECAUTIONS IN THE
MACHINE SHOP

(1) Be sure that all machines have effective and properly working guards that are always in place when machines are operating.

〔要點〕precaution 預防措施。machine shop 機械工場。Be sure that~ 查明……，確認……。properly 〔'prɑ(ɔ)pəli〕適當地。guard 〔gɑːd〕危險防止裝置，注意，用心。gaurd 後面的 that 是關係代名詞。in place 在正確的位置。

(2) Do not attempt to oil, clean, adjust or repair any machine while it is running. Stop the machine and lock the power switch in the "Off" position.

〔要點〕attempt 〔ə'tempt〕嘗試企圖（＝try）。　oil 加油（動詞）　adjust 〔ə'dʒʌst〕調節。repair〔ripεə〕修理。lock 按上，鎖上。the power switch 電源開關。off position 關的位置。

(3) Do not try to stop the machine with your hands or body.

(4) Always see that work and cutting tools on any machines are clamped securely before starting.

〔要點〕see that~檢查……，注意……。work 工作物。clamp: 夾緊。securely 〔si'kjuəli〕確實地。before starting（操作）開始前。

(5) Keep the floor clear of metal chips or curls and waste pieces.

Put them in the container provided for such things. Scraps are tripping hazards, and chips or curls may cut through a shoe and injure the foot.

〔要點〕 keep clear of～ 清理……。 chip 〔tʃip〕 破片，碎片。 curl 〔kə:l〕 （金屬的）彎曲的東西，指切屑。 waste pieces 廢品。 trip 拌倒。 hazard 〔'hæzəd〕 危險。 provided for＝that is provided for～ 為…… 而準備。 tripping hazards 容易拌倒的危險物。 injure 〔'indʒə〕 傷害。 cut through 割穿。

(6) All setscrews should be of flush or recessed type. If they are not, move with caution when near them. Projecting setscrews are very dangerous because they may catch on sleeves or clothing.

〔要點〕 setscrew 〔'setskru:〕 固定螺釘。 should be of～ 應該為……。 flush 〔flʌʃ〕 同一平面的。 recess 〔ri'ses〕 縮入。 projecting setscrew 突出的固定螺釘。 dangerous 〔'deindʒərəs〕 危險的。 may catch 有 拉住……之虞。 sleeve 〔sli:v〕 袖子。 clothing 〔'klouðiŋ〕 衣服。

(7) Get help for handling long or heavy pieces of material.

Follow safe lifting practices—lift with your leg muscles, not your back.

If you do not know how to lift safely, ask your foreman to show you.

〔要點〕 get help 請求幫助。 handle 處理。 material 〔mə'tiəriəl〕 材料， 物質。 follow 〔'fɔlou〕 遵從。 safe lifting practice 安全的抬高（物 品）方法。 muscle 〔'mʌsl〕 肌肉。 back 背。 how to lift 如何抬高。 ask your～to show 請求你的……示範。

(8) Do not run in the shop; there should be no "fooling around" in the shop at any time. Don't be a "wise guy."

Concentrate on the work and do not talk unnecessarily while operating a machine.

〔要點〕 fooling around 晃蕩。浪費時間之事。 at any time 任何時候。 guy 〔gai〕男人，人 (美國俗語)。 wise guy 聰明人。 concentrate 〔'ka(ɔ)nsentreit〕全神注意，集中。 unnecessarily 〔ʌn'nesisərili〕不必要的。 while operating a machine 當操作機器時。

(9) Don't talk to others when they are operating a machine.
(10) Get first aid immediately for ANY injury.
(11) Be sure you have sufficient light to see clearly. Check with the foreman if you do not have enough.

〔要點〕 first aid 〔fəːst eid〕應急處置 (急救)。 immediately 〔im'iːdiətli〕立刻。 injury 〔'indʒəri〕傷害。 any 任何的，很少地，輕微的。 sufficient 〔sə'fiʃənt〕充分的。 check 〔tʃek〕檢查。

(12) Always wear safety glasses, goggles, or face shield designed for the type of work when operating any machine.
(13) Wear clothing suited for the job. Wear shoes with thick soles—safety shoes if heavy work is being done.

〔要點〕 safety glasses 安全眼鏡。 goggles 〔'gaː(ɔ)glz〕保護眼鏡。 face shield 面罩 (焊接作業用，面部保護面具)。 suit 〔suː(juː)t〕適合。 suited for ～ 適合於 (＝which is suited for～)。 job 〔dʒa(ɔ)b〕工作。 thick 〔θik〕厚的。 sole 〔soul〕鞋底。 is being done 被做，從事 (現在進行的被動態)。

〔練　習　十二〕

A.　請把下列句子用英文寫出來:

1. 請注意操作

　注意 with care

2. 請小心脚步

　脚步 your step

3. 不要倚靠機器

　倚靠 lean 〔li:n〕 against

4. 請把所有鐵屑放入鐵屑箱

　鐵屑箱 scrap box。放入 put in一。

5. 工廠通道爲了避免跘倒或其他事故，請隨時保持清潔。

　工廠 shop, factory, works。通路 aisle 〔ail〕。爲了避免 to avoid。隨時 at all
　times, always。保持清潔 clean. clean up。

B.　請把下列英文翻譯出來;

1. Put tools away when not in use.

　put away整理。not in use不使用時。

2. Store materials in such a way that they cannot become tripping hazards.

　store貯藏。in such a way that 用這樣的方法。

2. PRODUCING STEEL by THE BESSEMER PROCESS

(14) In the Bessemer Process, the egg-shaped converter is charged with molten pig iron.

Air is blasted upward through the molten iron from tiny jets in the lower part of the converter.

〔要點〕 producing 生產 (動名詞)。　producing steel 製鋼。　Bessemer process 貝塞麥煉鋼法 (英人 Sir Henry Bessemer (1813-98) 發明的製鋼法)。egg-shaped 卵形的，　converter 轉爐。　charge 裝入。molten pig iron 熔化的生鐵。blast 吹氣，噴氣。upward 〔'ʌpwəd〕向上。molten-iron 熔鐵，鐵水。tiny 〔'taini〕非常小。jet 噴口。the lower part 下部。

(15) This oxidizes the carbon, manganese, and silicon, essentially removing them.

After 20 minutes the converter is charged with carbon and manganese, in the form of coke and Spiegeleigen (an alloy of iron and manganese), to bring the concentration of these elements to the desired amount.

〔要點〕 oxidize 〔'ɑ(ɔ)ksidaiz〕使氧化。essentially 〔i'senʃəli〕本質的，主要的。removing them 把它們除去 (remove 〔ri'muːv〕取去，除去)。in the form of～ 以……的形狀。spiegeleigen 〔'spiːgəlaizən〕鏡鐵 (德文，硬白生鐵)。concentration 集中，集結，濃縮。desired amount 所要的量 (desire 〔di'zaiə〕所望)。

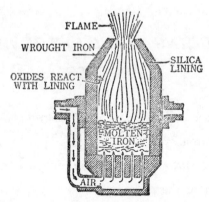

FLAME

WROUGHT IRON

SILICA
LINING

OXIDES REACT
WITH LINING

MOLTEN
IRON

AIR

The Bessemer Converter

(16) The air mixes the ingredients in a short time, and the converter is then tilted and the steel is poured into molds.

Bessemer steel has the lowest quality, and contains both sulfer and phosphorus.

〔要點〕 ingredient 〔in′griːdiənt〕成分，原料，要素。in a short time 在短時間內。 tilt 〔tilt〕傾倒。 is poured into～注入……之中 (pour 〔pɔː,pɔə〕注入)。mold 〔mould〕鑄模，模子 Bessemer steel 貝塞麥鋼。

(17) Sulfur causes steel to be brittle when hot (called *red short*), and phosphorus causes it to be brittle when cold (called *cold short*).

Bessemer steel is used in applications where the steel is subject neither to corrosive influences nor to shock.

〖要點〗 causes～to be brittle 把～脆化 (cause 〔kɔːz〕把……，變爲……的原因)。brittle 〔′britl〕脆。 red short 高溫脆性。 cold short 常溫脆性， application 〔æpli′keiʃən〕應用，使用。 where……的地方。 is subject 〔′sʌbdʒikt〕to 受到……。 corrosive 〔kə′rousiv〕腐蝕

生的。 influence 〔'influəns〕 影響。 shock〔ʃɑ(ɔ)k〕 衝擊。 neither 〔niː(ai)ðə〕 ~nor~……既不……也不……(在兩方面皆否定的情況下使用)

有關製鋼的術語

1. Bessemer Process (貝塞麥法): 又稱轉爐製鋼法, 英人 Henry Bessemer 發明的製鋼法, 把熔融的生鐵 (molten pig iron) 放入稱之為轉爐的卵形爐, 從爐上吹入高壓氧氣。利用生鐵中不純物氧化時的熱為燃料精煉鋼的方法。這種方法有酸性法 (acid process) 與鹼性法 (basic process) 兩種, 其製品稱為貝塞麥鋼 (Bessemer steel) 被用來作為快削鋼及鋼軌, 鎖, 鍛接管等。

2. Open Hearth Process (平爐製鋼法): 又稱西門斯—馬丁法 (Siemens-Martin Process) 因為爐形扁平所以有這種名稱。把生鐵, 鐵屑, 其他材料放入長方形反射爐 (reverberatory furnace) 加熱熔解製鋼。把製品稱為平爐鋼 (open hearth steel, siemens-Martin steel) 被用來製造較高級的鋼料。

3. Electric Process (電氣製鋼法): 使用電氣爐 (electric furnance) 的製鋼法, 一般電爐式的艾魯式電氣爐 (Heroult furnance) 與誘導式高週波電氣爐 (high frequency furnace) 廣泛被使用着, 因為能充分除去不純物, 所以適合合金鋼 (alloyed steel, alloy—) 等高級鋼的製造。

4. Crucible process (坩堝製鋼法): 把金屬放入坩堝用坩堝爐 (crucible furnance) 加熱使熔解均一的方法。因為鐵水不與燃燒氣體直接接觸, 所以可得品質好的東西, 適合製造工具鋼 (tool steel) 合金鋼等。

3. INTERNAL-COMBUSTION ENGINES

(18) The word "internal-combustion" means "inside-burning"——that is, the fuel is burned inside the cylinders.

Internel-combustion engines use the same source of energy as steam-engines and steam turbines.

〔要點〕 internal-combustion 內部燃燒。 inside burning 在裡面燃燒。 that is 則，卽，於是。 burn 〔bə:n〕燃燒。 the same source of energy as ～與……相同的能源。

(19) The most outstanding application of internal-combustion engines is for transportation——in cars, trucks, airplanes, and ships. In all these cases simplicity of operation and light weight are the deciding factors.

〔要點〕 outstanding 〔aut′stændiŋ〕顯著的，突出的。 truck 〔trʌk〕貨車。 simplicity 〔simp′lisiti〕輕便，簡易。 light weight 輕量。 deciding factor 決定因素。 decide 〔di′said〕決定。 factor〔′fæktə〕因素，要素。

(20) **Method of Charging.** In regard to the method of charging the cylinder, all engines can be divided into two groups, four-stroke and two stroke engines, depending upon the number of strokes required for completion of one cycle.

〔要點〕 method 〔′meθəd〕方法。 charging 供氣，供料（氣，油）。 in regard to～關於。 can be divided into～可分爲。 four-stroke 四衝程。 two stroke 二衝程。 depending upon 視……而定。 the number of strokes 衝程數。　completion 〔kəmp′liːʃən〕完成。　cycle 〔′saikl〕周期。

(21) **Fuel.** The fuel of an internal combustion engine is usually divided into three kinds, according to whether they operate on gaseous fuel, liquid fuel, or solid fuel.

【要點】according 〔ə′kɔːdiŋ〕to~ 根據~。　gaseous 〔′gæsiəs〕氣體的。whether 〔′hweðə〕or~還是……。

(22) Liquid-fuel engines can be subdivided into those using volatile fuels, such as gaoline or alcohol, and those using heavy oil; the first vaporizes the fuel by a carburetor, and their method of operation is very similar to that of gas engines.

【要點】subdivide 〔sʌbdi′vaid〕細分。　volatile 〔′vɑ(ɔ)ləti(ai)l〕揮發性的。vaporize 〔′veipəraiz〕使氣化。carburetor 〔′kɑːbjureitə〕氣化器，油化器。is very similar to~ 與……非常相似。similar 〔similə〕相同，頗似的。to that of gas engines 引擎的那個（方法）。

(23) In heavy-oil engines the fuel is injected into the air charge toward the end of the compression stroke.

These engines can be divided into low-, moderate-, and high-compression engines.

【要點】inject 〔in′dʒekt〕注入，噴射。　air charge 供氣。　compression stroke 〔kəm′preʃən strouk〕壓縮衝程。moderate 〔′mɑ(ɔ)dərit〕普通的，中等的。high compression engine 高壓縮引擎。

〔練習　十三〕

請把下列句子用英文寫出

1. 內燃機的燃料是從一般的石油得到的液體。
2. 在二衝程引擎中周期是二衝程卽機軸一回轉而完成

二衝程引擎: two stroke-cycle engine。機軸 crankshaft 〔′kræŋkʃɑːft〕。一回轉 one revolution。完成 complte.

有關內燃機的術語

內燃機 (internal-combustion engine) 係在汽缸 (cylincler) 內，將空氣與混合的燃料爆發燃燒，使活塞 (piston) 來回運動 (reciprocating motion) 的熱引擎 (heat engine)。根據活塞的衝程 (stroke) 分成 4 衝程 (foure cycle) 及二衝程 (two cycle) 兩大類，又根據使用燃料可分成氣體引擎 (gas engine)，汽油引擎 (gasoline engine)，重油引擎 (oil engine)，噴射燃料的，重氣點火引擎 (electric ignition engine)，柴油引擎 (Diesel engine) 及氣體渦輪 (gas turbine) 等。上述大多數使用於汽車，卡車，飛機，船舶等。

4. MECHANICAL DRAWING

(24) Engineering work of all kinds starts in the drafting room. Here the designers are worked out and the necessary drawings are made and checked.

〔要點〕 mechanical drawing 〔mi'kænikəl 'drɔːiŋ〕機械製圖。 engineering 工業上的，工程，工程學。 drawing 製圖，藍圖。 start in~始於。 work out 計劃，努力獲致。designer〔di'zainə〕設計者。 drafting room〔'drɑːftiŋ rum〕製圖室。 (= drawing office)。of all kinds 各種的 (= all kinds of~)。

(25) The subject of mechanical drawing is of great importance to all machinists, designers, and engineers.

　　Drawing is a method of showing graphically the minute details of machinery and apparatuses. so it is called the "engineer's language".

〔要點〕 graphically〔'græfikəli〕線圖，以圖解。 a method of showing~ 表示……的一種方法。 minute〔mai'njuːt〕微小的，細微的。 detail 〔'diːteil〕細部，零件圖。language〔'læŋgwidʒ〕語言。the egineer's language 工程人員的語言。

(26) In learning this language, we must learn what tools and instruments to use and how to use them skillfully, accurately, and quickly.

　　The drawing instruments used by draftsmen for producing pencil drawing are both varied and numerous.

〔要點〕 in learning this language 當學習這種語言時。　　what tools and

instruments to use 應該用什麼工具和儀器。 how to use 如何使用。 skillfully ['skilfuli] 精巧地。　accurately ['ækjuritli] 正確地。 quickly [kwikli] 迅速地。　drawing instrument 製圖儀器。　for producing 爲做出，爲繪出。　pencil drawing 鉛筆製圖。　varied ['vɛərid] 各式各樣的。 numerous ['nju:mərəs] 許多的。

(27) **Drafting machine** Drafting machines combine the functions of the T-square, triangles, scales, and protractor.

Lines can be drawn the exact lengths in the required places and at any angles by moving the scale ruling edge to the desired positions.

〔要點〕 drafting machine 製圖機械 (又稱爲 universal drafting machine) combine [kəm'bain] 組合。 T-square ['ti:skwɛə] 丁字尺。 triangle 三角規。　scale 刻度尺。　line can be drawn 線可被繪成。　exact [eg'zækt] 正確的。 at any angles 在任何角度。　scale ruling edge 刻度尺定向邊。 desired positions 希望的位置。

(28) This results in greater speed with less effort in making drawings. A complete understanding of efficient use, and care of the drafting machine will reveal its value.

〔要點〕 result in～ 引致，造成。　with less effort ['efət] 用少許努力，不太費力。 complete 完全的。 understanding [ʌndə'stændiŋ] 理解，知識。 efficient [i'fiʃənt] 有效的。 use 使用，利用。　care [kɛə] 注意，留心。 reveal [ri'vi:l] 顯示出，表現出。

(29) Drawing boards should be made of clear white pine, cleated

to prevent warping.

Care should be taken in their selection, the working edge should be tested with a steel straightedge.

〔要點〕 should be made of ～ 應由……做成。 clear 無色的。 white pine 白松。 cleat 〔kli:t〕 加上邊框。 prevent 〔pri'vent〕 防止。 warping 〔'wɔːpiŋ〕 彎曲，扭曲，起翹。 selection 〔si'lekʃən〕 選擇。 working edge 使用邊。 straightedge 〔'streitedʒ〕 直尺。

(30) Triangles are also called set-squares. They are made of various substances such as wood, celluloid, steel and plastics.

45° and 30°～60° triangles

〔要點〕 set-square 〔'set-skwɛə〕 三角板。
celluloid 〔'seljulɔid〕 賽璐珞。
plastics 〔'plæstiks〕 塑膠。

(31) Every draftsman should has at least two triangles, one having two angles of 45° and one right angle; and the other having angles of 30°, 60° and 90°, respectively.

〔要點〕 at least 至少。　one having ～ and the other having～ 一個有……而另一個有……。　respectively 〔ri'spektivli〕 分別地，各自地。

(32) **T-square** It consists of two parts—the head and the blade, and it is always used to draw horizontal lines.

the T-square

〔要點〕 head～ 尺頭。 blade 尺身。
horizontal line 水平線。

(33) **Working Drawings.** A working drawing is a drawing which completely describes the shape and size and gives specifications for the kinds of material, methods of finish, accuracy required and all the information necessary for making a complete machine or structure.

When completed, a working drawing must be thoroughly checked for errors and improvement.

〔要點〕working drawing 製作圖, 工作圖。 describe 〔dis′kraib〕描繪, 說明。 specification 〔spesifi′keiʃən〕規格。 finish 最後加工。 when completed＝when it is completed 當完成時。 thoroughly〔′θə:rouli〕完全地, 澈底地。 must be checked 必須加以檢查。 error 〔′erə〕錯誤。 improvement 改進, 改善。

(34) **Detail Drawings.** A detail drawing is a drawing which gives all the information necessary for making a single piece.

It is the simplest form of working drawing and must be a complete and accurate description of the piece.

〔要點〕detail drawing 分圖, 詳細圖。a single piece 單一物件 description 〔dis′kripʃən〕描寫, 說明。

(35) Sometimes separate detail drawings are made for the use of different workmen, such as the patternmaker, hammersmith, machinist, or welder.

〔要點〕separate 個別的, 不同的。are made for the use of～ 爲……的使用而作。 patternmaker 〔′pætənmeikə〕木模工。 hammersmith 〔′hæməsmiθ〕鍛造工。

(36) **Assembly Drawing.** A drawing of completely assembled construction is called an assembly drawing. Its particular value is to show that the parts go together and provides the appearance of the construction as a whole.

Assembly drawings are generally made to small scale.

〔要點〕 assembly 〔ə'sembli〕 drawing 裝配圖 (=assembling drawing)。
　　a completely assembled construction 完整裝配成的構造物。
　　particular 〔pə'tikjulə〕 特別的，特殊的。 is to show that～ 是表示
　　出……。 go together 結合，組合。 appearance 〔ə'piərəns〕 外表，外
　　觀。 as a whole 作爲整體。 small scale 縮小比例尺。

〔練 習 十四〕

將下文譯成英文:

1. 每一個製圖工至少應有一組製圖儀器。
　　一組製圖儀器 a set of drawing (或 drafting) instruments.

2. 丁字尺一般是用木材，賽璐珞或塑膠製成。

3. 分角器是測量角度用的器具。
　　angle 角度

4. 圓規用於繪出圖或圓弧。
　　compasses 圓規

5. 圖板一般用乾燥過及直木紋的軟松木製成。
　　乾燥過 well-seasoned。 直木紋 straight-grained。 松 pine。

5. GENERATORS

(37) There are only two important sources of electrical energy: cells and generators.

Cells are very convenient for many purposes, and we use them a great deal.

〔要點〕 generator 發電機。 cell 電池。 convenient 〔kən'viːnjənt〕方便的，便利的。 a great deal 大大的，大量的。

(38) But, as you know, the electrodes and electrolytes of cells are so expensive that it is not practical to use cells to supply current for lighting houses and streets, for heating purposes, and for running large motors.

〔要點〕 as you know 如你所知。 electrode 〔i'lektroud〕電極。 electrolyte 〔i'lektroulait〕電解物。 expensive 〔iks'pensiv〕價昂的。 so~ that~ 如此……以致……。 supply 〔səp'lai〕供應，供給。 for lighting 照明用。 heating purposes 加熱目的。 for running 運轉用。 motor 電動機，馬達。

(39) When large amounts of current are needed for a considerable length of time, generators are used.

There are large generators run by steam or moving water in electric power plants all over the world.

〔要點〕 large amounts of ~ 大量的。 length of time期間。 moving water 流水。 electric power plant 發電廠。

(40) Every airplane, modern ship, and nearly every factory has one or more generators run by an engine or motor.

The Diesel engines on streamlined trains and the steam turbines on many ships drive generators whose current transmits energy to the driving wheels or propellers.

〔要點〕 run by ＝which are run by～ 被……帶動。　streamlind 〔'stri:m laind〕流線形的。 driving wheel 〔'draiviŋ hwi:l〕主動輪。

(41) Generators are machines for producing electical energy. In other words, a generator changes mechanical kinetic energy into electrical energy.

One kind of generator designed to furnish large amounts of electrical energy is called the alternating-current generator, or altenator.

〔要點〕 machines for producing～ 生產……的機器。 in other words 換言之。 kinetic energy 〔ki'netik, 'enədʒi〕動能。 one kind of～ ……的一種。 furnish 〔'fə:niʃ〕供給。 alternator 〔ɔ:ltə:'neitə〕交流發電機。

(42) We often call it the AC generator, for short. In one sense, a magneto is an alternating-current generator, because it produces an alternating current.

AC generators consist of three essential parts:
1. The field magnet, which produces lines of force.
2. The armature, which consists of an iron core wound with a large number of coils of insulated wire.

〔要點〕 AC generators 〔ei si: 'dʒenəreitə〕直流發電機。 for short 簡略。

in one sense 就某種意義說。 magnetor 〔mæg′niːtou〕久磁發電機，磁電機。 field magnet 〔fiːld ′mægnit〕場磁。 which＝and it。 line of force 力線。 armature 〔′ɑːmətjuə〕電樞。 iron core 〔aiən kɔə〕鐵心。 wound 〔waund〕 wind 〔waind〕 (繞曲) 的過去分詞。 a large number of〜 許多的。 coil 〔kɔil〕 線圈。 insulated wire 〔′insjuleitid ′waiə〕 絕緣線。

(43) The armature revolves on an axis between the poles of the field magnet, and in so doing cuts magnetic lines of force.

3. The slip-rings and brushes.

All dynamos generate alternating current in the armature exactly as in the case of the single rotating loop.

〔要點〕 axis 〔′æksis〕軸，軸線。 pole 極。 in so doing 像那樣的。 magnetic lines of force 磁力線。 slip-ring 滑環。 brush 〔brʌʃ〕電刷。 dynamo (＝generator) 發電機。 as in the case of〜 如同……情形一樣。 single rotating loop (luːp) 單一旋轉環線。 (loop 環線)。

(44) When this current is taken from the armature by the brushes which rest on the slip-rings, the current in the external circuit is also alternating; that is,it flows through the external circuit first in one direction, and then in the opposite direction.

〔要點〕 rest 靜止，置於。 external circuit 外部廻路。 first in one direction 最初在一方向。 opposite 〔′ɔpəzit〕相反的。

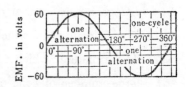

(45) Since there are two alternations for each revolution or cycle

of the armature, and many commercial machines have a frequency of 60 cycles per second, the number of alternations is 120 per second.

〔要點〕 alternation 〔ɔːltəːˈneiʃən〕 交替。commercial 〔kəˈməːʃəl〕 商業上的。
the number of alternations 交替數。

(46) For use in heating, lighting, and certain power purposes the alternating current is satisfactory; hence alternators are extensively used.

〔要點〕 heating 〔hiːtiŋ〕 加熱。　lighting 照明，點燈。　satisfactory 〔sætisˈfæktəri〕 滿意的，合宜的。hence 〔hens〕 因此。

(47) The parts of a DC generator are the same as those of an AC generator, with one exception: The collector contains a device called a commutator instead of slip-rings.

　The commutator changes the alternating current of the armature into a current which flows in one direction only in the external circuit.

〔要點〕 DC generator〔diːsiː ˈdʒenəreitə〕 DC 發電機。are the same as 與……同樣的。exception 〔ikˈsepʃən〕 例外，除外。collector 〔kəˈlektə〕 集流器，集電器。commutator 〔ˈkɔmjuteitə〕 整流子。instead of～ 代替。

(48) Such a current is called a direct current, a continuous current, or even better, a unidirectional current, to distinguish it from the alternating current.

〔要點〕direct current 〔′direkt ′kʌrənt〕直流電。　　continuous current 〔kən′tinjuəs ′kʌrənt〕連續電流。　　even better 甚而更佳。 unidirectional current 單方向電流。

(49) In its simplest form, the commutator consists of a ring of brass which has been split into two semicircular segments, carefully insulated from each other.

Brushes resting on these segments take current from them just as brushes do from the slip-rings of the alternator.

〔要點〕a ring of brass 黃銅環。　has been split 被分裂 (split 分裂，分割)。 segment 片，段。　carefully 〔′kɛəfuli〕謹慎地。　insulated 被絕緣。 brushes resting on~ 電刷置於……上。

有關發電機的術語

發電機 (electric generator dynamo) 是將機械動力轉換爲電力 (electric power) 的裝置之總稱。在磁場 (magnetic field) 內對固體導體作用運動磁場 而得感應電動勢 (induced electromotive force)。可大別爲交流發電機 (AC generator) 與直流發電機 (DC generator) 兩類，其根本上的發電作用則相同。

DC generator (DC 發電機)

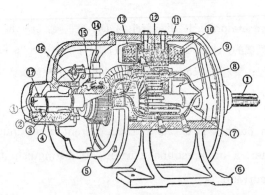

① shaft 軸 ② oil 油　③ oil ring 油環　④ bearing 軸承　⑤ commutator 整流子　⑥ bed, base 鐵台　⑦ armature coil 〔'ɑ:mətjuə kɔil〕電樞線圈 ⑧ end plate 端板　⑨ armature core 電樞鐵心　⑩ field core 磁場鐵心 ⑪ yoke 軛鐵 ⑫ field core 磁場鐵心 ⑬ field winding 磁場繞組 ⑭ brush 電刷 ⑮ brush holder 刷座 ⑯ brush rocker 電刷搖移器 ⑰ bearing metal 軸承金屬。

bipolar dynamo 〔bai'poulə 'dainəmou〕二極發電機

compound generator 〔'kɔmpaund 'dʒenəreitə〕複激發電機

multipolar generator 〔mʌlti'poulə 'dʒenəreitə〕多極發電機

polyphase generator 〔'pɔlifeis 'dʒenəreitə〕多相發電機

shunt generator 〔ʃʌnt 'dʒenəreitə〕分激發電機

series generator 〔siəri:z 'dʒenəreitə〕串激發電機

single-phase generator 〔'siŋgl-feis 'dʒenərəreitə〕單相發電機

synchronous generator 〔'siŋkrənəs 'dʒenəreitə〕同步發電機

three-phase generator 〔'θri:-feis 'dʒenəreitə〕三相發電機

two-phase generator 〔'tu:feis 'dʒenəreitə〕二相發電機

unipolar generator 〔ju:ni'poulə 'dʒenəreitə〕單極發電機

6. TOOTHED GEARS

(50) Belt, friction pulleys, and other types of power transmission that depend upon friction are subject to slippage and so do not transmit a definite and invariable speed ratio.

〔要點〕 toothed gear 〔tuθt giə〕 齒輪 (=toothed wheel)。 belt 帶。 friction pulley 〔'frikʃən 'puli〕 摩擦滑輪。　power transmission 〔'pauə træns'miʃən〕 動力傳遞。 depend upon 依靠。 are subject to~ 承受。　slippage 〔'slipeidʒ〕 滑動量。　transmit 〔trænz'mit〕 傳遞。

definite 〔'definit〕一定的。 invariable 〔in'vɛəriabl〕 不變的。 speed ratio 速率比。

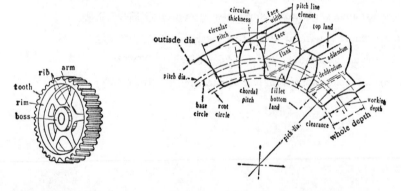

toothed wheel (齒輪)　　　terms used with gear teeth 用於齒輪齒部的術語。

(51) Chains and gears are used when positive drives are necessary, and where the center distances are relatively short, toothed gears are prefered. To prevent slipping, teeth are added to the wheels.

〔要點〕 positive drvie 〔'pozitvi draiv〕 確實的傳動。　center distances

中心距。add 〔æd〕加。

(52)　There are numerous kinds of gears, of which the most common forms are *spur gears* for transmitting power from one shaft to another parallel shaft, and *bevel gears* for two shafts whose axes intersect, usually at right angles.

〔要點〕 of which 在其中。the most common forms 最普通的式樣。 spur
　　　 gear 〔spəː giə〕正齒輪。 for transmitting power 傳達動力用的。
　　　 another parallel shaft 另一平行軸。bevel gear 〔'bevəl giə〕斜齒輪。
　　　 at right angles 直角。

(53)　Usually when one gear of a pair is much smaller than the other it is called a "pinion."

　　　The parts of gear teeth have names, as given in the above drawings.

〔要點〕 one gear of a pair 一對齒輪中的一個。 pinion 〔'pinjən〕小齒輪。
　　　 gear teeth（齒輪）的齒。in the above drawings 在上面的圖。

(54)　Gear Terms and Abbreviations.—The following information and formulas can be used to find required dimensions, etc., for standard gears:

〔要點〕 gear terms 齒輪用語。required dimensions 所要的尺寸。
　　　 standard gear 標準齒輪。

(55)　N＝number of teeth　　　A＝addendum＝$1/DP$
　　　D＝deddendum $1.157/DP$　　C＝clearance＝$0.157/DP$
　　　PD＝pitch diameter＝N/DP

OD＝outside diameter＝N＋2/DP＝2A＝PD

CP＝circular pitch＝πPD/N

DP＝diametral pitch＝N/PD

RD＝root diameter＝PD－2D

WD＝whole depth＝A＋D

〔要點〕 number of teeth 齒數。　　　addendum 〔ə'dendəm〕 齒冠 (複數爲 addenda 〔ə'dendə〕) deddendum 〔di'dendəm〕 齒根 (複數爲 deddenda 〔di'dendə〕)。clearance 〔kliərəns〕 間隙。pitch diameter 〔pitʃ dai'æmitə〕 節圓直徑。outside diameter 外徑。circular pitch 〔'sə:kjulə pitʃ〕 周節。　diametral pitch 徑節。root diameter 〔ru:t dai'æmitə〕 齒根直徑。

〔練 習 十五〕

把下列句子用英文寫出

1. 正齒輪是在適當的速度及正常的情況下最常用的工業機械。

適當速度 at moderate speeds。正常的情況下工作 working under ordinary conditions。工業機械 industrial machines

2. 歪齒輪用以連接兩個不相交的軸

它的軸不相交 whose axes do not intersect

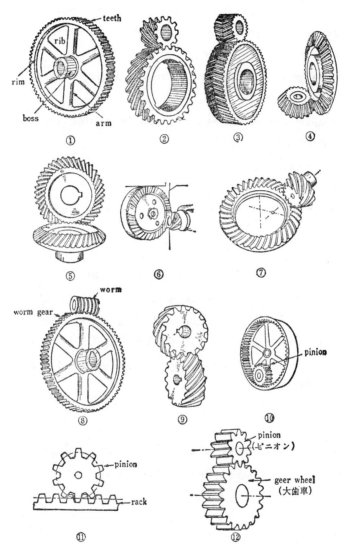

Various kinds of Ge   (各種的齒輪)

① spur gear 正齒輪 ② helical gear 螺旋齒輪 ③ double-helical gear 双
螺旋齒輪 ④ straight bevel gear 直斜齒輪 ⑤ spiral bevel gear 蝸旋斜齒

輪 ⑥ skew bevel gear 歪斜齒輪 ⑦ hypoid gear 戟齒輪 ⑧ worm and worm gear 蝸桿及蝸輪 　 ⑨ screw gear 螺輪 　 ⑩ internal gear 內齒輪 ⑪ rack and pinion 齒條及小齒輪 ⑫ gear wheel 大齒輪。

Easy Ways to Calculate Pulley Sizes and Shaft Speeds.

IF YOU KNOW

Speed and diameter of driving pulley, and diameter of driven one

AND WANT

Speed of driven pulley

DO THIS

Multiply speed of driver by its diameter; divide by diameter of driven pulley

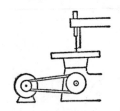

EXAMPLE: A 2″ motor pulley turns at 1,750 r.p.m. to drive a 3 1/2″ pulley on a jigsaw. How many strokes a minute will result? Multiply 1,750 by 2; divide by 3 1/2. Answer: 1,000.

IF YOU KNOW

Speed and diameter of driving pulley and required speed of driven one

AND WANT

Diameter of driven pulley

DO THIS

Multiply speed of driver by its diameter; divide by required driven speed

EXAMPLE: A counter-shaft is to turn at 1,650 r.p.m. when driven from a 3″ pulley on a gas engine governor-controlled at 2,200 r.p.m. What size pulley is needed on the countershaft? Multiply 2,200 by 3; divide by 1,650. Answer: 4″.

IF YOU KNOW

Required speed and diameter of driven pulley, and speed of driving shaft

AND WANT

Diameter of driving pulley

DO THIS

Multiply required speed of driven pulley by its diameter; divide by speed of driving shaft

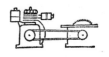

EXAMPLE: A cut-off wheel to run at 4,000 r.p.m. has a $1^3/_4''$ sheave on its arbor. What size driving pulley is needed on a 1,750-r.p.m. motor? Multiply 4,000 by $1^3/_4$; divide by 1,750. Ans.: $4''$.

IF YOU KNOW

Diameters of both pulleys and required speed of driven shaft

AND WANT

Speed of driving shaft

DO THIS

Multiply diameter of driven pulley by the required speed; divide by diameter of driving pulley

EXAMPLE: A gas engine with a $3''$ pulley is to drive a circular saw at 3,600 r.p.m. The saw shaft has a $2^1/_2''$ pulley. At what speed must the engine run? Multiply 3,600 by $2^1/_2$; divide by 3. Answer: 3,000 r.p.m.

上文是美國的通俗機械雜誌 Popular Mechanics 中 "V Belts and their Drives（V 形皮帶及其傳動）中所刊登，文章的簡易說明如下:

〔解說〕Easy ways to calculate pulley sizes and Shaft speeds. 計算滑輪大小及軸速的簡易方法，標題分成 IF YOU KNOW 如果知道，AND WANT 要知道，DO THIS 像這樣做（DO LIKE THIS 的意思）等幾個項目。

driving pulley 主動滑輪。 driven one = driven pulley 從動滑輪。multiply~by~ 以……相乘。divided by~ 以……相除。example 例子，實例。

r.p.m. =revolutions per minute 每分鐘轉數。 jigsaw 狹條鋸， How many strokes a minute will result? 一分鐘的行程是多少？required speed 所要求的速度。countershaft 〔'kauntəʃɑːft〕副軸。is to turn at 以……轉運。when driven from a 3″ pulley 由3″的滑輪運轉時。gas engine 氣體引擎(＝gasoline engine) governor-controlled 〔'gʌvənə-kən'trould〕調速機控制。 driving shaft 主動軸。sheave 〔ʃiːv〕槽輪。arbor 〔'ɑːbə〕(＝arbour) 心軸。circular saw 〔'səːkjulə sɔː〕圓鋸。

7. WELDING

(56) Welding is being used for an everincreasing variety of mechanical and structural purposes, such as building up and fastening parts together.

Welding has become common practice for steel buildings.

〔要點〕 welding 焊接。is being used 被用 (現在進行被動式)。
everincreasing 〔evəinˊkriːsiŋ〕一直增加着。building up 組合。
fastening parts together 將零件連接。has become common practice
已成爲常用方法。steel building 鋼鐵建造物。

(57) Steel shapes, plates, and bars may be welded together to make machine frames, bases, jigs and fixtures, and so forth.

Since steel is approximately six times as strong in tension as cast iron and two and one-half times as stiff, it is apparent that by using steel greater strength and rigidity may be secured with less weight of metal.

要點〕 steel shape 型鋼。 may be welded together 可被焊接在一起。
machine frame 機械骨架。 jig and fixture 冶具及夾具。 and so
forth ……等。 approximately 〔əˊprɔksimeitli〕 約 (=about)
tension 〔ˊtenʃən〕拉力。cast iron 鑄鐵。stiff 〔stif〕强, 硬。it is
apparent that 那是明顯的。 rigidity 〔riˊdʒiditi〕剛性。 may be
secured 可被確保 (secure 〔siˊkjuə〕確保)　 with less weight of
metal 更輕的金屬。

(58) Sheet-metal work, such as tanks and other containers, can

be simplified by welding instead of riveting the joints.

The aircraft, automotive, and shipbuilding industries **have** developed welding as a major fabricating method for aluminum and magnesium, as well as for steel.

〔要點〕 sheet-metal work 板金加工。container 容器。can be simplified 能被簡化。 riveting 〔'rivetiŋ〕鉚釘固定。 joint 〔'dʒɔint〕接頭。automotive 〔ɔ:tə'moutiv〕汽車的。shipbuilding industries 造船工業。 have developed 已發展。(develop 〔di'veləp〕發展) major 〔'meidʒə〕大部分的，主要的。fabricating method 製造方法，組合方法 (fabricate 〔'fæbrikeit〕製造，組合)。as well as for steel 如同鋼鐵一樣。

(59) **Welding processes.** The two basic processes are fusion welding and resistance welding. Fusion welding makes use of welding material in the form of a wire or rod which is added to the weld. These filler rods combine with the metal being welded.

〔要點〕 welding process 焊接方法。fusion welding 融化焊接。resistance welding 電阻焊接。makes use of～ ～利用……。welding material 焊接材料。 in the form of ……的形狀。 in added to～ 被加到。filler rod 填充棒材，熔填材料。combine with～ 與……混合。 **the metal being welded** 被焊接金屬。

(60) Gas or a carbon arc is used to create the heat so that **the** metals flow together.

Resistance welding uses an electric current to generate welding heat by the resistance of the parts to an electric current. The parts are welded by pressure.

〔要點〕carbon arc 碳弧。 create〔kriéit〕產生。 so that the metals flow together 使金屬流在一起（so that ⋯⋯使之）。welding heat 焊接熱。

(61) Welding processes include forge welding, resistance welding, arc welding, gas welding, thermit welding, induction welding, cold welding, and soldering and brazing.

Types of joints are shown and named in the following figures. There are many variations in the kinds of welds used in making these joints.

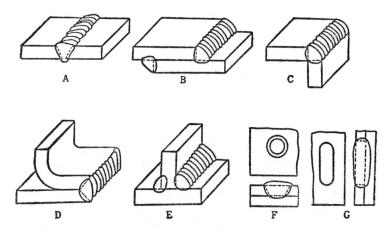

Basic types of joints.
(A) Butt joint (V-groove weld). (B) Lap joint (fillet weld).
(C) Corner joint (fillet weld). (D) Edge joint (V-groove weld)
(E) T-joint (fillet welds). (F) Plug weld. (G) Slot weld.
Basic types of joints（接頭的基本形式）

A對接接頭	B搭疊接頭	C角綠接頭
D邊綠接頭	E T型接頭	F塞焊
G槽塞焊		

〔要點〕include〔in'klu:d〕含，包含。 forge welding 鍛接。arc welding 電弧焊接。 thermit〔'θə:mit〕welding 發熱焊接。 induction welding 感應焊接。 cold welding 壓接。 brazing〔'breiziŋ〕硬焊。 figure

圖，圖形。 variation 〔vɛəriéiʃən〕 變化，不同的。 in the kinds of weld 焊接的種類。

〔練　習　十六〕

把下列句子用英文寫出：

1. 機械的底座，骨架及托架是由焊接接合形鋼及板金所組合而成。

　機械的底座 machinery base。 型鋼 shape steel。 板金 plate。 組合而成 are built up。

2. 焊接越來越廣泛使用於永久結合方法，以取代往日被使用的鉚釘和螺栓。

　往日的 formerly。 被使用的 were employed。 永久結合方法 permanent fastening 〔'fæsniŋ〕。 越來越…… more and more, gradually

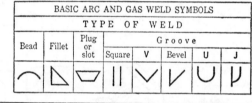

（美國焊接協會之焊接記號）

主要的焊接方法表

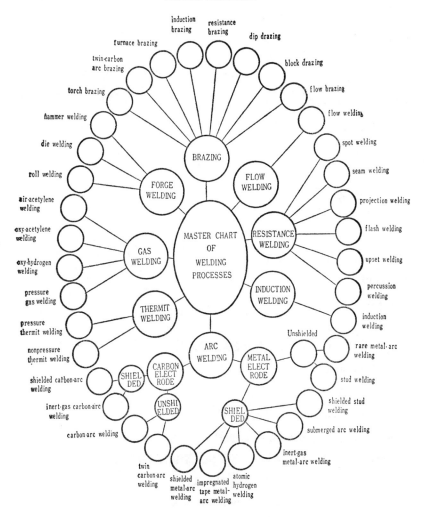

Master chart of welding process（主要焊接方法圖表）

brazing 銅焊

　　torch brazing 銲炬式銅焊

　　twin-carbon arc brazing 双碳極電弧銅焊

    furnace brazing 熱爐式銅焊

    induction brazing 感應式銅焊

    resistance brazing 電阻式銅焊

    dip brazing 浸焊式銅焊

flow welding 熔燒焊接

resistance welding 電阻焊接

    spot welding 點焊焊接

    seam welding 縫合焊接

    projection welding 突壓焊接

    flash welding 閃衝焊接

    upset welding 對衝焊接

    percussion welding 碰撞焊接

induction welding 感應焊接

arc welding 電弧焊接

metal electrode 金屬電極

unshielded 不遮蔽的

    rare metal-arc welding 稀有金屬電弧焊接

    stud welding 螺樁焊接

shielded 遮蔽的

    shielded stud welding 遮蔽螺樁焊接

    submerged arc welding 潛弧焊接

    inert-gas metal-arc welding 不活性氣體金屬電弧焊接

    atomic hydrogem welding 原子氫焊接

    impregnated tape metal-arc welding 滲入式金屬電弧焊接

    shielded metal arc welding 遮蔽金屬電弧焊接

carbon electrode 碳電極

    twin carbon-arc welding 双碳極電弧焊接

    carbon arc welding 碳極電弧焊接

inert gas carbon-arc welding 不活性氣體碳極電弧焊接

shield carbon-arc welding 遮蔽碳極電弧焊接

thermit welding 發熱焊接

nonpressure thermit welding 不加壓發熱焊接

pressure thermit welding 加壓發熱焊接

gas welding 氣體焊接

pressure gas welding 加壓氣體焊接

oxy-hydrogen welding 氧氫氣體焊接

oxy-acetylene welding 氧乙炔氣體焊接

air acetylene welding 空氣乙炔氣體焊接

forge welding 鍛接

roll welding 輥軋鍛接

die welding 模壓鍛接

hammer welding 鍛錘鍛接

8. THE AIRCRAFT INDUSTRY

(62) An aircraft includes many different kinds of parts of many different materials. There are also many differdnt methods of making the parts and putting them together.

〔要點〕 aircraft 〔'ɛəkrɑːft〕 航空機。 part 零件。 putting them together 將
　　　　零件組合 (put together 組合)

(63) There is the fuselage or central body of the airplane which contains the operating and passenger compartments.

〔要點〕 the fuselage or central body 機的中心或本體。
　　　　passenger 〔'pæsindʒə〕 乘客，旅客。

(64) The fuselage may have welded truss construction (a rigid welded frame-work) or a metal skin braced on the inside. There are wings which are built of welded light metal ribs covered with metal sheets (skin).

〔要點〕 may have ……將會有。 welded truss construction 熔接的構架構造。
　　　　a rigid welded framework 固定熔接的骨架。 metal skin 金屬面板。
　　　　braced 支持，使固定。 are built of ~ 用……建造。 welded light metal
　　　　rib 焊接之輕金屬骨架。 metal sheet 薄金屬板。

(65) Different methods are used for fastening the wings to the fuselage. A wing is called an airfoil. Other support surfaces termed airfoils include ailerons, elevators, and rudders.

〔要點〕 for fastening 爲了固定。 airfoil 〔ɛə'fɔil〕 翼面。 support surfaces 支

持面。termed＝named。aileron 〔'eilərɔn〕副翼。elevator 昇降舵。
rudder 方向舵。

(66) A chord is a straight line between the leading edge and the
trailing edge. Elevators, ailerons, rudders, tabs and flaps are used to
control the airplane in flight.

〔要點〕chord 翼弦。leading edge 〔'li:diŋ edʒ〕前緣。trailing edge 〔'treiliŋ
edʒ〕翼的後緣。tab 〔tæb〕補助翼 (昇降舵) 後端的小翼。flap〔flæp〕
襟翼，下翼。flight 〔flait〕飛行。

(67) There is an undercarriage to absorb the shock of landing.
There is the power plant, either piston-type engines or jet engines,
and an arrangement for mounting and transmitting power.

〔要點〕undercarriage 〔'ʌndəkæridʒ〕(飛機的) 着陸裝置 (＝leading gear)。
absorb 〔əb'sɔ:b〕吸收。landing 着陸。power plant 動力發生裝置。
piston-type engine 活塞式引擎。　　jet engine 噴射式引擎。
arrangement 〔ə'reindʒmənt〕配置。mounting 〔'mauntiŋ〕裝置，
安裝。transmitting power 動力的傳遞 (＝transmission of power)。

(68) Of course, there are fuel tanks, electric circuits, lubricating
systems, control-operating mechanisms, and so forth.
All of this means that different kinds of industry take part in
making an airplane.

〔要點〕lubricating system 〔'lu:brikeitiŋ 'sistim〕滑潤系統。　　control-
operating mechanism 操縱機構。take part 參與。

(69) Some parts are made in different plants and have to be fitted
as the plane is assembled.

Some parts have to be laid out on sheets of metal or scribed from templates.

〔要點〕 have to be fitted 必須被裝配。　have to be laid out 必須被佈置 (lay out 設計，佈置)。scribe from……從……劃線。scribe〔skraib〕劃線。template〔'templit〕型板（＝templet〔'templet〕）

(70) Casting, forging, welding, riveting, and other methods of forming and construction are used in the making of an airplane.

The aircraft industry continually tries to improve its methods in order to manufacture aircraft more efficiently at lower cost.

〔要點〕 casting 鑄造。　forming 成形。　in the making of 在製造……中。continually〔kən'tinjuəli〕連續的。　improve〔im'pru:v〕改良。in order to 爲了。　efficiently 有效的。

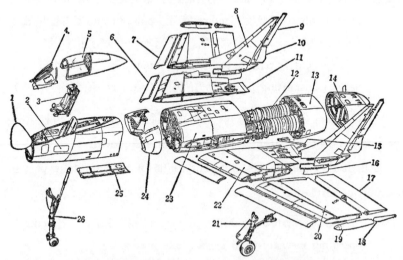

An exploded view of a two-engine jet-propelled airplane
（双引擎噴射推進式飛機之分解零件配置圖）
exploded view〔iks'plɔ:did vju:〕分解零件配置圖

jet-propelled 〔dʒet-prə'peld〕噴射推進式的

①radome 〔'reidoum〕雷達圓頂

②fuselage front section 機體前部斷面

③ejection seat 〔i'dʒekʃən siːt〕射出座位

④windshield 〔windfiːld〕遮風玻璃

⑤cockpit canopy 〔'kɔkpit 'kænəpi〕駕駛室天蓋

⑥conter section slat 翼心條板

⑦outer panel slat 外側機翼條板

⑧fin 〔fin〕直尾翼

⑨rudder 方向舵

⑩auxiliary rudder 補助方向舵

⑪speed brake assembly 速度刹車組件

⑫jet engine 噴射引擎

⑬fuselage aft section 機體後部

⑭tail cone 機尾椎體

⑮arresting hook 〔ə'restiŋ huk〕速度控制裝置

⑯main landing gear door 主着陸裝置門

⑰ailavator 〔ei'læveitə〕補助翼

⑱ailavator tip 補助翼端

⑲wing tip 〔wiŋ tip〕翼端

⑳wing outer panel 〔wiŋ'autə 'pænəl〕外側機翼

㉑main leading gear 主着路裝置

㉒wing center section 翼心斷面

㉓fuselage mid-section 機體中心部斷面

㉔engine air intake duct 發動機進氣導管

㉕nosegear door 降落裝置門

㉖nose gear 降落裝置

〔練　習　解　答〕

〔練習一〕

1. 10+7=17

   Ten and seven are seventeen.　Ten and seven make seventeen.

   Ten plus seven equals seventeen.

2. 15−11=4

   Eleven from fifteen leaves four.　Fifteen minus eleven is four.

   Fifteen minus eleven equals four.

3. 80×4=320

   Four times eighty is three hundred and twenty.

   Four times eighty make three hundred and twenty.

   Eighty multiplied by four equals three hundred and twenty.

4. 13.3+3=16.3

   Thirteen (decimal) point three and three make sixteen (decimal) point three.

   Thirteen (decimal) point three plus three equals sixteen (decimal) point three.

5. 80/4=20

   Eighty over four is (or equals) twenty.

〔練習二〕

(A) 80°F eighty degrees F (或 Fahrenheit)

   155°F a (or one) hundred and fifty-five degree F (Fahrenheit)

   18°C eighteen degrees C(或 centigrade)

   98°C ninety-eight degrees C(或 centigrode)

(B) 1. 溫度或以華氏或以攝氏被測定。

   2. 在攝氏刻度冰點在零度，沸點在 100 度處。

　　3. 另一方面在華氏刻度冰點在32°，沸點在212°處。

（C）1. On the fahrenheit scale the boiling point is marked 212°

　　　2. While on the centigrade scale the boiling point is marked 100°

〔練習三〕

1. One inch equals 2.54　centimeter (cm).

2. Engineering units are all based upon (or on) the Metric system.

3. The Metric system of weights and measures is used in all scientific work.

〔練習四〕

1. 多少立方厘米的軟木與1立方厘米的黃金同樣重量。

2. 汽車用蓄電池中的酸，當電池完全充電時有1.28之比重。

3. 上表中的那一個物質浮在水上。

〔練習五〕

1. 如已知，歐姆定律的公式表示電流的流動 E. M. F 之比率與電阻之間的關係。

2. 電動馬達的動力常稱之爲馬力，所以有時候需要把馬力換算爲瓦特或千瓦特。

〔練習六〕

1. My house stands on a hill.

2. My uncle's house consists of two stories.

　　或 My uncle's house has two stories.

3. Who lives downstairs?

4. Do you sleep upstairs?

〔練習七〕

A 1. Copper is one of the most useful metals.

　2. Copper is applied to many domestie purposes.

　3. Brass is an alloy of copper and zinc.

B 1. 銅廣泛使用於管道工作，自來水管及烹飪具。

　2. 其美觀，使其更廣泛的用於裝飾用。

〔練習八〕

A 1. A tanker is an huge floating tank built to carry oil and other fluids.

2. The engines are located at the rear of the ship.

B 1. 油輪為了防止火災以及避免船貨移動，分成兩個劃區。

2. 在船尾有供船員們吃睡的甲板室。

〔練習九〕

1. 自動化何時被介紹到美國汽車工業？

2. 自動化的原理並不新穎，約 175 年前的連續製粉機的製作，即為其最初期的應用之一。

3. 設計自動控制方式並不一定像看見的那麼容易。

〔練習十〕

1. 原子是能顯出元素特性的元素的最小粒子。

2. 原子的原子序數是圍繞原子殼內電子之和。

3. 原子的原子量是原子核內的質子與中子數的和。

4. 元素記號表示元素的名稱，元素的一原子以及元素的一原子量的值。

〔練習十一〕

1. 技術人員目前正在實驗不從煤炭或燃料而從稱為原子爐的機器得到熱量的一種新型蒸氣機。

2. 約60年前科學家們知悉原子不是單一的塊狀而是恰巧像行星圍繞太陽一樣，由相互旋轉的微小粒子所組成的複雜的小群。

〔練習十二〕

A 1. Handle it with care. 或 Treat it with care.

2. Watch your step.

3. Don't lean against the machines.

4. Put all scrap in scrap boxes. 或 Please put ～.

5. Aisles in the shop should be (或 must be) clean (up) at all tines (in order) to avoid tripping and other accidents.

B 1. 當不使用的時候把工具收拾好。

  2. 用不會成爲易眸倒之危險物的方法貯存材料。

〔練習十三〕

1. The fuel of an internal-combustion engine [is usually a liquid obtained from petroleum.

2. In a two stroke-cycle engine the cycle is completed in two strokes, or one revolution of the crankshaft.

〔練習十四〕

1. Every draftsman should have at least a set of drawing instruments.

2. T-squares are usually (或是 generally) made of wood, celluloid or plastics.

3. The protractor is an instrument for measuring angles.

4. The compasses are used for making circles and arcs.

5. The drawing board is usually made of well-seasoned and straight-grained soft pine.

〔練習十五〕

1. Spur gears are most commonly found on industrial machines. working under ordinary conditions at moderate speeds.

2. Skew bevel gears may be used to connect shafts whose axes do not intersect. (may be used=can be used)

〔練習十六〕

1. Machinery bases, frames and bracket are built up of steel shapes and plates joined by welding.

2. Welding is being used more and more extensively for permanent fastenings in places where formerly rivets or bolts were employed (extensively=widely, employed=used).

〔研究編譯文〕

1. 機械工廠內的安全預防措施

（1）　確信機械在運轉的時候，所有機械均具有有效與適切的防止危險裝置並且安置在適當位置。

（2）　當機械在運轉中不可加油，清掃，調整，或修理，應停開機械把電源開關按在"關"的位置。

（3）　不要試着用你的手或身體使機械停止。

（4）　在開動前要檢查裝在機械上的工作物及刀具，是否確實的夾緊。

（5）　清除地板上的金屬碎片或彎曲碎屑，以及廢品，保持乾淨。把它們放入預備好的容器之中。廢鐵是使人踦倒的危險物，金屬破片或彎曲碎屑也許會割穿鞋底損傷腳部。

（6）　所有的固定螺釘應該用平頭或縮入型，假如不是的話，靠近的時候應加注意。突出的固定螺釘因爲有拉住衣袖或衣服之虞，是很危險的。

（7）　搬運長或重的工料時，請人幫助，遵從安全的抬高操作方式—用你的腳部肌肉而不是用背部抬高。

假如你不曉得如何安全的抬高，請求你的領班加以示範。

（8）　不要在工廠內奔跑，任何時候在工廠內不應有"晃蕩"之事，不要作所謂的"聰明人"，操作機械時全神集中於工作，不要說不必要的話。

（9）　當別人在操作機械時不要對別人說話。

（10）　對任何人的傷害，應立刻請求緊急救護。

（11）　確認你有充分的光線，看得很清楚（物件），假如光線不夠的話告訴領班。

（12）　當操作機械時，經常戴上因工作性質而設計的安全眼鏡，保護眼鏡或面罩。

（13）　穿上適於工作的衣服，假如笨重的工作在進行，穿上厚鞋底的鞋子——安全鞋。

2. 貝塞麥法的煉鋼

（14）　貝塞麥法是把熔融的生鐵注入卵形的轉爐中，空氣從轉爐下部微小的噴口向上吹送，通過鐵水。

(15)　這（空氣）使碳，錳以及矽氧化，主要是爲除去它們。20分鐘後將碳與錳以焦碳及鏡鐵（鐵和錳的合金）的形態裝入轉爐，使這些元素達到所需求的濃度。

(16)　空氣在短時間內，使諸成分混合，然後將轉爐傾斜，鋼水卽被注入鑄模之中。貝塞麥鋼，品質最差，含有硫和磷。

(17)　硫在加熱時引起鋼的脆化（稱爲熱脆性）。而磷在冷却時引起鋼的脆化（稱爲冷脆性）。貝塞麥鋼使用於鋼料不受腐蝕，也不受衝擊影響之場所。

3. 內　燃　機

(18)　"內燃"這話指"內部燃燒"卽燃料在汽缸內被燃燒。內燃機使用與蒸氣機及蒸氣渦輪機同樣的能源。

(19)　內燃機最顯着的應用爲運輸用如汽車，貨車，飛機以及船舶。所有這些場合裡，操作簡單及輕便是決定性的因素。

(20)　**供氣方法**　關於汽缸供氣的方法，所有引擎可區分爲兩組，卽 4 衝程及 2 衝程引擎，乃視完成一周期所需衝程數而定。

(21)　**燃料**　內燃機的燃料，根據操作時用氣體燃料，液體燃料還是固體燃料，分成三種。

(22)　液體燃料引擎能細分爲使用揮發性燃料者，如汽油或酒精，以及使用重油者。第一者（揮發性燃料）用化油器使燃料氣化，而其操作方法與氣體引擎的方法極爲相似。

(23)　重油引擎的燃料是在壓縮衝程將近結束時，噴入供氣中，這些引擎可分成低壓，中壓及高壓壓縮引擎。

4. 機　械　製　圖

(24)　所有工程上的工作都始於製圖室。在這裏設計者計劃及將必要的藍圖繪製並加以校核。

(25)　機械製圖之科目對所有機械師，設計師和工程師都很重要。製圖是用線圖表示機械和裝置細部的一種方法。所以稱爲"工程人員的語言"。

(26)　當學習這種語言時，我們必須學會應使用那些工具和儀器，並且如何精巧，正確和迅速的使用它們。繪圖者爲繪製鉛筆藍圖所用的製圖儀器，種類多數目也多。

(27) **製圖機械**　製圖機械是結合丁字尺，三角規，刻度尺和分角器的功用。可以移動刻度尺的定向邊至所需的位置，而在所需要的地方及任意的角度繪出正確長度的線。

(28) 結果造成繪圖時，速度更快而又不太費力。對製圖儀器完全瞭解並小心有效的使用，方可發揮出其價值。

(29) 製圖板應以白松木製成，並加上邊框以免彎曲。

選擇製圖板時，應注意。使用邊應以鋼製直尺檢驗。

(30) Triangles（三角規）也稱為 "set-squares" 它可用數種物質做成。如木材，賽璐珞，鋼和塑膠。

(31) 每一個製圖者，至少應有兩個三角板，一個有兩個45°角，另一個為直角，而另一個分別有30°，60°和90°的角。

(32) 丁字尺，由兩個部分組成——尺頭與尺身，而它是常用以繪製水平線。

(33) **製作圖**　描繪製作圖是為製造一完整的機械或構造物而完整地說明其形狀，尺寸並賦予材料種類之規格，加工的方法，需要精度，以及所有必須資料的一種圖。

當完成時製作圖必需澈底地加以檢查錯誤並加以改正。

(34) **分圖**　分圖是製造單一物件，而附有所需資料的圖。

它是最簡單形式的製作圖，但必須對該物件做完整及正確的說明。

(35) 有些時侯，為了不同工作人員的使用，諸如木型工，鍛造工，機械工或焊接工，特各別的繪製。

(36) **裝配圖**　一個構造物完整裝配成的圖卽稱為裝配圖。

其特殊價值是表示出各部分結合情形和顯示結構物的整個外觀。

裝配圖一般是以縮小比例尺繪製。

5. 發　電　機

(37) 電能僅有兩種重要的來源：電池和發電機。

在許多用途上，電池是很方便的，所以我們用的很多。

(38) 但是如你所知，電池的電極和電解液是如此價昂，以致實用上不能用電池供應電流做為房屋和街道照明用，加熱目的和轉動大型馬達。

(39)　當相當長期間需要大量電流時，則使用發電機。

在全世界上，有許多發電廠之大型發電機是以蒸汽或水力轉動。

(40)　每一飛機，現代化的船隻，以及幾乎每一個工廠都有一個或更多的引擎或馬達帶動的發電機。

流線型火車上的柴油引擎和許多船上的蒸汽渦輪機係用來驅動發電機，其電流把能量輸送至主動輪或推進器。

(41)　發電機是產生電能的機器。

換言之，發電機將機械動能轉換為電能。

有一種發電機設計用來供給大量電流的，被稱為交流發電機，或交流機。

(42)　我們經常簡略稱它為 AC 發電機，就某種意義言，磁電機就是一種交流發電機，因其產生交流電。

AC 發電機由三主要部分組成

①場磁，其產生(磁)力線。

②電樞，其由許多絕緣線之線圈所纏繞的鐵心組成。

(43)　電樞繞場磁之兩極間的軸線旋轉，並因此而切斷磁力線。

③滑環和電刷

所有的發電機，在電樞上產生交流電流的情形，如單一旋轉環線一樣。

(44)　當電流自電樞被置於滑環上的電刷帶走時，在外面線路上的電流也是交流的，也就是說，它流經外面線路時，最初是在一方向而後在另一方向。

(45)　由於電樞每轉一圈或一循環有兩次交變，而許多商業上的機器有每秒60循環的頻率，所以交變數為每秒120次。

(46)　在加熱，照明和某些特定動力用途上的使用，交流電是令人滿意的，因之，交流發電機使用很廣泛。

(47)　DC 發電機之組件與 AC 發電機者相同，唯一例外為集流器上，含有整流子的裝備以取代滑環。

整流子將電樞上的交流電改變為僅在外面線路電流為單向流動。

(48)　如此的電流被稱為直流電，一連續電流或更佳者稱為單一方向電流，以與交流電區別。

(49) 它的最簡單形式，整流子是由一被分裂爲二半圓片而有良好絕緣的黃銅環構成。就如同交流發電機之電刷由滑環帶走電流一樣，電刷置於半圓片而帶走電流。

6. 齒　　　輪

(50) 皮帶，摩擦滑輪及其他根據摩擦來傳遞動力的方式，易滑動而無法獲得一定及不變的速率比。

(51) 鏈條及齒輪使用於需要確實傳動時，但中心距比較短的地方多用齒輪，爲了防止滑動，輪上加齒。

(52) 齒輪有多種，其中最普通的形式爲正齒輪，用於從一軸傳達動力到另外一個平行軸上，以及斜齒輪使用於兩個軸線相交的軸，通常是直角（相交）。

(53) 通常，一對齒輪中一個比另一個小很多的齒輪稱爲"小齒輪"。齒輪的齒各部分的名稱，如上面的圖所示。

(54) **齒輪用語與略語**——下面的資料及公式常用在算出標準齒輪所要的尺寸及其它事項。

(55) $N=$齒輪的齒數　　　　$A=$齒冠$=1/DP$

$D=$齒根$=1.157/DP$　　　$C=$間隙$=0.157/DP$

$PD=$節圓直徑$=N/DP$

$OD=$外圓直徑$=N+2/DP=2A=PD$

$CP=$周節$=\pi PD/N$

$DP=$徑節$=N/PD$

$RD=$齒根直徑$=PD-2D$

$WD=$全深度$=A+D$

7. 焊　　　接

(56) 焊接被用於一直增加的各種機械及架構上的目的，例如各種組合及零件的連接。

焊接已普遍的應用於鋼鐵建造物。

(57) 型鋼，板金及棒材可焊接接合以製造機械的骨架，底座，冶具，及夾具等等。

因爲鋼比鑄鐵有 6 倍的抗張强度，二倍半的剛度，故明顯的藉鋼的高强度
及剛性，可用較少重量的金屬以保安全。

(58)　板金加工，例如槽及其它容器，接頭，能藉焊接代替鉚釘而簡化
航空機械，汽車及造船工業，利用鋁及鎂的焊接，如同鋼一樣已發展爲主
要的製造方法。

(59)　**焊接方法**　兩個基本的方法是融化焊接及電阻焊接。融化焊接是在焊接部
加上線狀或棒狀的焊接材料，這種塡裝棒材與被焊接金屬熔合。

(60)　氣體或碳弧常被用於產生熱能使金屬流在一起，
電阻焊接 使用電流藉焊接部分之電阻產生焊接熱能，焊接部分焊接時要
加壓力。

(61)　焊接方法，包含鍛接，電阻焊接，電弧焊接，氣體焊接，發熱焊接，感應焊
接、冷焊，及軟焊和硬焊。
接頭的形式及名稱如下圖所示。　可用許多不同的焊接方式以製造那些接頭。

8.　航空機械工業

(62)　一架飛機包括許多種不同材料的許多不同種類的零件，零件的製造及組合
也有很多不同的方法。

(63)　飛機機體的中心或本體包括操作房及旅客室。

(64)　機體有焊接之構架，（剛强的焊接構架）或金屬面板固定在內面，有用輕
金屬焊接之骨架外覆上薄金屬板建造的機翼。

(65)　機翼與機體連接的方法有很多種，機翼被稱爲翼面 (airfoil)，其他支持
面稱爲翼體組，包括副翼，升降舵及方向舵。

(66)　翼弦是機翼，前緣與後緣之間的一條直線。升降舵，副翼方向舵，補助翼，
及下翼，常用於控制飛行中的飛機。

(67)　有着陸裝置以吸收着陸時產生的震動，有活塞式引擎或是噴射式引擎的動
力發生裝置，並有裝置及傳遞動力的裝配。

(68)　當然，有燃料箱，電氣回路，潤滑系統，操縱機構等等，以上卽表示有不
同種類的工業參與製造飛機。

（69）　某些零件是由不同的工廠製造，在裝配飛機時必須被組合完成，某些零件
　　　　必須被設計成片狀或是用型板劃線。

（70）　鑄造，鍛造，焊接，鉚接及其他成型及建造方法常被用於製造飛機。
　　　　航空機工業一直努力，嚐試更有效率及價格低廉之航空機械製造法。

參 考 編

1. 工業英文法的概要

　　研讀英文必須熟悉英文法 (English Grammar)。英文法係有系統的學習單語組合及文章構造的學科，所以對英文法沒有心得時無法正確的翻譯英文或寫作英文。尤其是工業英文 (Engineering English) 具有與普通的英文稍異的獨特文章構造及用法。

　　工業用文例如原書、型錄、廣告文以及解說書，技術報告等，與普通的散文或小說大異其趣，要求的是簡單明瞭，所以自然而然大量的使用分詞形，動名詞將文章縮短成單文，同時也利用略語略字。這是工業文的一大特徵。因此本編的重點在於說明理解工業文最起碼的文法基本知識，至於與工業文沒有密切關係的假定法等則盡量省略，使讀者能夠從本編能學到工業英文譯讀的要領與實力。

　　什麼叫詞類 (Parts of Speech)

　　所有的文 (Sentence) 係將語 (word) 在一定的規則下組合而成。語在文章中所演的角色稱爲詞類，共有如下的 8 種，所以稱爲 8 大詞類(The Eight parts of Speech).

　　1. 名詞　　2. 代名詞　　3. 形容詞　　4. 動詞　　5. 副詞
　　6. 前置詞　　7. 連接詞　　8. 感嘆詞

I.　名詞 NOUN

　　表示人、物、事名的語，有以下的 5 種。

①專有名詞 (Proper Noun) 僅此一個的名詞。人名、地名、公司名、工廠名等。
　Edison (愛廸生), London (倫敦), General Electric Company (通用電氣公司)

　〔注意〕專有名詞必須以大寫開頭。

②普通名詞 (Common Noun) 共同用於同類事物之名。

bolt (螺釘), engineer (工程師), car (汽車), signal (信號)

③集合名詞(Collective Noun) 表示集合點之名。

ironworks (鐵工廠), firm (商行), class (班級), group (團體)

④物質名詞 (Material Noun) 表示物質, 材料之名。

water (水), iron (鐵), glass (玻璃), oil (油)

⑤抽象名詞 (Abstract Noun) 表示性質、狀態、動作之名。

drive (駕駛), safety (安全), work (工作)。

(1) 名詞之單數及複數

①單數名詞 (表示一個事物之名)

a nut (1 個螺帽), an engine (1 台引擎), a shaft (1 根軸)

②複數名詞 (表示二個, 或二個以上事物之名)

two nuts (2 個螺帽), five engines (5 台引擎), ten shafts (10根軸)

(2) 複數名詞之造法

①普通取〔單數名詞＋ s〕之形。

單數	複數	
watt	watts	瓦特
pipe	pipes	管
hammer	hammers	鐵鎚

②單數名詞的語尾係s, x, ch, sh 等時取〔單數名詞＋es〕之形。

單數	複數	
glass	glasses	玻璃杯
box	boxes	箱
switch	switches	開關
brush	brushes	刷子

③單數名詞的語尾係〔子音＋y〕時變y為 i 並 es。

單數	複數	
body	bodies	本體
battery	batteries	電池

company   companies   公司

但是單數名詞的語尾係〔母音＋y〕時只加 s 。

chimne<u>ys</u> 煙商   allo<u>ys</u> 合金   pulle<u>ys</u> 滑輪

④單數名詞的語尾係 f 或 fe 時變為 v 並加 es

單數	複數	
knife	knives	刀
leaf	leaves	葉

〔例外〕roofs。屋頂。chiefs 主任、課長。

⑤單數名詞的語尾係 is 時成為 es。

單數	複數	
analysis	analyses	分析
basis	bases	基礎
axis	axes	軸
hypothesis	hypotheses	假設

但 chassis（框架，底盤）單・複同形。

⑥母音 oo 變成 ee 者。

單數	複數	
foot	feet	英尺
tooth	teeth	（齒輪的）齒

⑦外來英文的單數及複數

單數	複數	
addendum〔ədéndəm〕	addenda〔ədéndə〕	齒尖
antenna〔ænténə〕	antennae〔ænténi:〕	天線
apparatus〔æpəréitəs〕	apparatuses〔æpəréitəsiz〕 apparati〔æpəréiti:〕	裝置
datum〔déitəm〕	data〔déitə〕	資料
deddendum〔dedéndəm〕	deddenda〔dedéndə〕	齒根
focus〔fóukəs〕	foci〔fóusai〕	焦點

formula 〔fɔ́:mjulə〕	formulas 〔fɔ́:mjuləz〕 formulae 〔fɔ́:mjuli:〕	公式
medium 〔míːdjəm〕	mediums 〔míːdjəmz〕 media 〔míːdjiə〕	媒介物
phenomenon〔finɔ́minən〕	phenomena 〔finɔ́minə〕	現象
radius 〔réidiəs〕	radii 〔réidiɑi〕	半徑

⑧常取複數形的名詞

　ⓐ由兩個部分組成的器具名。

　　pincers 鉗子　　dividers 分割器　　tongs 夾具　　scales 天秤

　　shears 剪斷機　　scissors 剪刀

　ⓑ學科名

　　aeronautics 航空力學　　dynamics 力學　　electronics 電子工學

　　hydraulics 水力學　　mathematics 數學　　mechanics 機械學

　　physics 物理學

⑨複數形時意思會改變的名詞。

　　casting 鑄造 ⟶ castings 鑄件

　　physic 醫學 ⟶ physics 物理學

　　compass 羅盤 ⟶ compasses 兩脚規

　　work 工作 ⟶ works 工廠

⑩物質名詞數量的表示方法

　　a sheet of paper　　1張的紙

　　five tons of coal　　5噸的煤

⑪複數形 s 的省略（名詞具有形容詞的功用時）。

　　a five-tube set 5燈收音機

　　a 100-watt bulb 100瓦特燈泡

(3) 名詞之所有格

①人（特別是原理，法則，方式等的發見者，訂定者）之名加……'s，此 s 稱爲
　所有格符號（Apostrophe—s）

Boyle's law 波義耳定律

Einstein's Theory of Relativity 愛因斯坦之相對性原理

Newton's Laws of Motion 牛頓之運動法則

the machinist's trade 機械工的職業

語尾已有 s 時只加……'

Plumbers' supplies 鉛管工的供給

engineers' English 工程師的英文

②無生物名詞所有格之表示法〔所有物＋無生物名詞〕

the end of the rope 繩索的末端

the grates of the boiler 鍋爐的火格子

the pressure of the air 空氣的壓力

the windings of the motor 馬達的線圈

(注意) of 前之名詞大約都加 the

③無生物在以下的場合也可加……'s, ……s'。

a machines' life 機械的壽命 (時間)

thirty miles' power transmission 30哩的電力輸送 (距離)

ten meters' length 10公尺的長度 (距離)

a kilogram's weight 1 公斤的重量 (重量)

④爲加强語氣有時用二重所有格

a photograph of our manager's 我們的經理的相片 (相片的所有人也是
經理的時候)

a photograph of our manager 我們的經理的相片 (相片的所有人不明的
時候)

⑤同格名詞 (Appositive Noun) 二名詞並列而後名詞說明前名詞時，後名詞與
前名詞同格，稱爲同格名詞。

Mr. Chen, our engineer, is very famous.

我們的工程師陳先生非常有名。

II.　代名詞 PRONOUN

代替名詞之語。有人稱代名詞，指示代名詞，疑問代名詞，關係代名詞4種。
此地只說明與工業用文較有關係的疑問代名詞及關係代名詞。

(1)　疑問代名詞　(Interrogative Pronoun)

表示疑問之意的代名詞。用於單、複數的人、物、事等

用 法 ＼ 格　數	單　數・複　數　同　形		
	主　　格	所　有　格	受　　格
人	who　（誰）	whose　（誰的）	whom（誰）
人、物	what　（什麼）	——	what（什麼）
人、物	which　（那個）	——	which（那個）

Who are you? 你是誰？

Whose is this spanner? 這起子是誰的？

Whom do you want to see? 你想見誰？

What is that? 那是什麼？

Which is your drawing pencil? 哪一枝是你的製圖鉛筆？

Which of you can solve this problem? 你們那一個能解決這問題？

(2)　關係代名詞　(Relative Pronoun)

代替名詞（或代名詞），並同時連結前後的語句。

A.　例如① I have many workmen. 我有很多員工。

　　② They work very hard. 他們很認眞工作。

上面二文中②之 They 以 who 取代與①連結而成：

I have many workmen. They work very hard.

我有許多的員工，他們很認眞工作。

I have many workmen **who** work very hard.

我有許多很認眞工作的員工。

He has a micrometer. It is very accurate.

他有一支分厘卡，其是很準確。

He has a micrometer **which** is very accurate.

他有一支很準確的分厘卡。

上面兩文中的 who, which 等稱爲關係代名詞，將前面的 workmen. micrometer 稱爲先行詞 (Antecedent).

B.　Here is an apprentice. His name is Chen.

此有一學徒，他的名字是陳。

Here is an apprentice **whose** name is Chen.

此有一姓陳的學徒。

此時 whose 是關係代名詞，其先行詞是 apprentice.

C.　Here is an engineer. I kno him well.

此有一位工程師，我知道他很清楚。

Here is an engineer **whom** I know well.

此有一位我知道很清楚的工程師。

這時的關係代名詞爲 whom，先行詞爲 engineer.

上面例文中A的 Who 代替 They（主格）並連結上下句自成爲連接詞，所以屬於主格的關係代名詞；B 的 Whose 具有 His（所有格）及連接詞的功用，所以屬於所有格的關係代名詞；又C的 Whom 有 Him（受格）及連接詞的功用，稱爲受格的關係代名詞。

①關係代名詞的種類及變化（單・複同形）

用法 ＼ 格	主　　　格	所　有　格	受　　　格
用　　於　　人	who	whose	whom
用　於　人　以　外　之　物	which	whose, of which	which
用　於　所　有　的　東　西	that	――	that
先行詞＋關係代名詞	what	――	what

②who 的用法

ⓐ主格時

He is a skilled designer **who** made this engine.

他是一位熟練的設計人員，其製成此引擎。

（他是一位製成此引擎的熟練設計人員）

ⓑ受格時

Mr. Chen is the young fracer **whom** l know.

陳先生是一位年青描圖員，我知道他。

（我知道陳先生是一位年青描圖員）

ⓒ所有格時

He is a welder **whose** name is called Chen.

他是一位焊接員，他的名字被叫做陳。

（他是一位被叫做陳的焊接員）

③**which** 的用法

ⓐ主格時

That is the factory **which** belongs to Mr. Chen.

那個是工廠，它屬於陳先生的。

（那個是屬於陳先生的工廠）

（which 是 factory 的 代名詞而是 belong 的主語）

ⓑ受格時

This is the new vice **which** I made

這是新的老虎鉗，它是我做的。

（這是我做的新老虎鉗）

（which 代表 vice，成為動詞 made 的受詞）

ⓒ所有格時

This is the chisel the top **of which** is broken.

這是鑿子，它的頂部是被弄破了。

或 This is the chisel **whose** top is broken.

這是頂部被弄破的鑿子。

④ **that** 的用法

可用於任何先行詞的很方便的語。主格、受詞都可用，但無所有格。

ⓐ主格時

I know the engineer **that** teaches you mathematics.

我知道一位工程師，其教你數學。

(我知道教你數學的一位工程師)。

(that 代表 engineer, 成爲動詞 teaches 的主語)。

ⓑ受格時

This is the television **that** he made.

這是一台電視機，其由他所做成的。

(這是他做成的一台電視機)。

(that 代表 television, 成爲動詞 made 的受詞)

ⓒ先行詞是 all, any, only, first, last. the same, 最高級等，必須用 that.

This is all **that** I brought.

這是全部，我所帶來的。

(這是我所帶來的全部)

I will give you any tool **that** you like.

我將給你任何工具，那是你所喜歡的。

(我將給你任何你所喜歡的工具)。

This is the only meter **that** l have.

這是唯一我所有的量器。

James Watt is the first man **that** invented a steam engine.

詹姆士瓦特是發明蒸氣機的第一人。

This is the best measuring instrument **that** I could find.

這是我能找到最好的測量儀器。

This is the Same tape. **that** l lost.

這是與我所遺失相同的錄音帶。

(注意) This is the same tape **as** I lost.

這是正如我所遺失的錄音帶。

⑤ **what 的用法**

與 who, which, that 不同，係沒有先行詞的特別的關係代名詞，但具備〔先行詞＋關係代名詞〕的意思。

This is the switch **which** (或 that) I made＝This is **what** I made.

這是我所做的開關＝這是我所做的。

He always forgets **what** he learns.

他總是忘記他所學的。

I can make **what** he designs.

我能做出他所設計的。

⑥附有前置詞的關係代名詞

the house **in which** I live

這房子我住的。

（我住入的房子）

the pencil **with which** I was drawing

這支鉛筆是我用做劃圖的。

（我用做畫圖的鉛筆）

the hole **through which** the fuel passes out.

此孔讓燃料流出。

（使燃料流出的孔）

the furnace **at which** the gas and air are entering.

爐子正通進煤氣及空氣。

（正通入煤氣及空氣的爐子）。

the rate **at which** the magnetic field produced by the input coil.

輸入線圈感應所產生的磁場變率。

an arrangement **in which** an oscillating detector is employed.

一個裝置，於其中使用着振動檢波器

（使用着振動檢波器的一個裝置）。

the casing **within which** the turbine revolves.

一個箱蓋，其裡面輪機旋轉着 。

（輪機旋轉於箱蓋內）。

he first invention **of which**……

他最初發明東西中的……

engine, **in which** the heat is supplied within the cylinder.

引擎，在其中熱被供應到氣缸內。

（熱被供應到引擎的氣缸內）。

the material **upon which** this industry depend.

此材料其爲這種工業所依賴。

（這種工業所依賴的材料）。

⑦關係代名詞的兩種用法

ⓐ限定用法 (Restrctive Use)……引導形容詞子句。

We engaged Mr. Chen **who** is gas turbine expert.

我們約定陳先生，其爲氣輪機專家。

（我們約定氣輪機專家陳先生）。

It was the first engine **that** could go faster than the horse.

那是第一個引擎，它能跑得比馬快。

（那是第一個能跑得比馬快的引擎）。

Are there any meter **that** you want **which** you have not?

有沒有你要的量器呢？但那是你沒有的。

ⓑ連續的用法 (Continuous Use)……可代以〔連接詞＋代名詞〕

I met a skilled mechanic, **who** (=and he) showed me how to read a micrometer.

我遇到一位熟練員工，他教我如何讀分厘卡。

We have the underground railway, **which** (=and it) will. be extended in the near future.

我們此處有地下鐵道，其不久將被延長。

⑧關係代名詞的省略

關係代名詞爲受格而限定用法時常省略。

I have polished up the roll 〔that: which〕 you order me yesterday.

我已拋光你昨日命令我作的輥子。

This is the machine 〔that: which〕 I made.

這是我做的機械。

III.　形容詞 ADJECTIVE

修飾名詞表達其性質，狀態等的語，有下列兩種修飾法。

ⓐ直接修飾（形容詞直接在名詞的前面）

This is a **useful** instrument. 這是很有用的器具。

ⓑ間接修飾（形容詞在述部）

That hammer is **heavy.** 那鐵鎚很重。

(註) 有的形容詞只能用在名詞前面。

the **latter** half 後半, the **inner** tube 內胎（車胎的）。

the **outer** wall 外壁, the **following** table 次表。

形容詞的種類　形容詞有以下的 4 種。

(1) 性質形容詞 (**Qualifying Adjective**)

修飾名詞敍述其性質、狀態者。大部分的形容詞屬於此類。

economical materials 經濟的材料, the **effective** life 有效壽命。

A mechanical engineer 機械工程師, **American** products 美國產品。

(2) 代名形容詞 (**Pronominal Adjective**)

從代名詞轉化者。

this lathe 這車床, **that** shaft 那軸。

此外有 another, such, each, every, any, these, those 等。

(3) 疑問形容詞 (**Interrogative Adjective**)

代名形容詞的一種，本身爲疑問詞兼作形容詞之用。

what crane 什麼起重機, **which** vice 那一個鉗子。

(4) 數量形容詞 (Quantitative Adjective)

表示數、量等的形容詞。

many workers 多數的工人 ⎫
few designer 少數的設計員 ⎬……數

much power 多量的動力 ⎫
little paint 少量的油漆 ⎬……量

慣用句

a great many ~ ⎫
a good many ~ ⎬非常多數的……（數）
a large number of ~ ⎭

a great deal of ~ ⎫
a good deal of ~ ⎬非常多量的……（量）
a large quantity of ~ ⎭

其他 a lot (of) ~（或 lots of ~）可用於數及量兩方面。

(5) 形容詞的配列順序

①普通照如下的次序，但例外也很多。

數量＋形態＋性質＋名詞

a large type centerless grinder 大型的無心磨床

two horizontal type milling machine 兩台橫式銑床

many hexagon headed black bolts 多數的六角黑頭螺釘。

much effective current 多量的有效電流。

this new belt 這新的皮帶。

②特殊者

all 隔 the 修飾名詞。

all the oil ＝ the whole oil 全部的油。

其他

opposite direction ＝ the direction **opposite** 反對的方向

a half ampere 或 **half** an ampere $1/2$ 安培

（也可只稱 **half** ampere）

(6) 數詞 (Numerals)

數量形容詞之中表示定數的語，有下列兩種。

基數 (cardinal numbers)		序數 (ordinal numbers)	
1 one	2 two	1st the first	2nd the second
3 three	4 four	3rd the third	4th the fourth
5 five	6 six	5th the fifth	6th the sixth
7 seven	8 eight	7th the seventh	8th the eighth
9 nine	10 ten	9th the ninth	10th the tenth
11 eleven		11th the eleventh	
12 twelve		12th the twelfth	
13 thirteen		13th the thirteenth	
14 fourteen		14th the fourteenth	
15 fifteen		15th the fifteenth	
16 sixteen		16th the sixteenth	
17 seventeen		17th the seventeenth	
18 eighteen		18th eighteenth	
19 nineteen		19th the nineteenth	
20 twenty		20th the twentieth	
21 twenty-one		21st the twenty-first	
22 twenty-two		22nd the twenty-second	
30 thirty		30th the thirtieth	
40 forty		40th the fortieth	
50 fifty		50th the fiftieth	
90 ninety		90th the ninetieth	
100 one (a) hundred		100th the hundredth	
153 one hundred and fifty-three		153rd the one hundred and fifty-third	
500 five hundred		500th the five hundredth	
999 nine hundred and ninety-nine		999th the nine hundred and ninety-ninth	

（註）ⓐ上表中有下線者注意拼字與發音。

ⓑ基數13～19的語尾爲—teen, 20～90的語尾爲 ty。

ⓒ20以上的十位數加上一位數時要用連字號 (hyphen) 連接。

〔例〕twenty-five HP. (25馬力)，eighty-five meters (85公尺)

ⓓhundred 之後有數字時以 and 連接。

〔例〕one hundred and forty volts (140伏特)。

ⓔ序數要加 the. 序數用於日期，階級等表示順序者。

〔例〕Feb. 11th (讀成 February (the) eleventh) 2 月11日

The Second power plant. 第二發電廠

The Third Law of Motion 運動之第三法則

但也可用基數代替序數。

The Second power Station = No. 2 power station

the fifth page = page five.

the eighth part = part eight.

ⓕ千以上的基數

1,000 (千) one (a) thousand

10,000 (萬) ten thousand

100,000 (十萬) one hundred thousand

1,000,000 (百萬) one million

10,000,000 (千萬) ten million

100,000,000 (一億) one (a) hundred million

8,123,456 (八百十二萬三千四百五十六)

eight million, one hundred and twenty-three thousand, four hundred and fifty-six

十億以上的大數目英美的表示法不同

	英 式	美 式
十 億	one thousand million	one billion
百 億	ten thousand million	ten billion
千 億	one hundred thousand million	one hundred billion
一 兆	one billion	one trillion

ⓖ倍數詞 (Multicative number) 的表示方法

the **double** capacity of manager and chief-engineer

　　經理兼主任工程師的双重資格。

double the monthly salary　2倍的月薪。

half the sum 半額, three **times**　3倍。

ⓗ其他

200V. two hundred volts 200伏特

5KWH. five kilowatt-hours 5千瓦時。

32°F. thirty-two degrees Fahrenheit 華氏32度

27°C. twenty-seven degrees Centigrade 攝氏27度

58% fifty-eight per cents 百分比58

羅馬數字

羅　馬　數　字	阿拉伯數字	羅　馬　數　字	阿拉伯數字
I	1	XXX	30
II	2	XL	40
III	3	XLI	41
IV 或 III	4	L	50
V	5	LX	60
VI	6	C	100
VII	7	CL	150
VIII	8	CC	200
IX	9	D	500
X	10	M	1,000

　　（註）羅馬數字的V=5, X=10, L=50, C=100, D=500, M=1,000在這些記
　　　　號的左側有數字時爲"－", 右側有數字時爲"＋"。例如IV=4, VI=6 等。

(7) 比較 (Comparison)

　　比較事物的性質、狀態、表示及程度的形容詞功用稱爲比較，有下列3種。

①原級 (Positive Degree) 不與他物比較單獨使用。

②比較級 (Comparative Degree) 用於比較兩者。

③最高級 (Superlative Degree) 用於比較三個以上。

〔例〕 This sheet steel is **light**.（原級）

　　This sheet steel is **lighter** than that sheet steel.（比較級）

　　This sheet steel is the lightest of all steet sheet.（最高級）

　　(sheet steel 薄鋼板，最高級必須加 the)

(8) 比較級的作法

(1) 照規則變化者。

　　原級＝形容詞原形。　比較級＝原級＋er.　最高級＝原級＋est.

原　　　　級	比　較　級	最　高　級	語　尾　的　變　化
强的 strong	stronger	strongest	加-er,-est
大的 large	larger	largest	語尾 e 時加-r,-st.
薄的 thin	thinner	thinnest	語尾子音重覆再加-er,-est.
重的 heavy	heavier	heaviest	語尾的 y 變成 i 再加-er,-est

　　但是原級由二音節以上構成時照下面的規則。

　　比較級＝more＋原級　　最高級＝most＋原級

原　　　　　級	比　較　級	最　高　級
有用的 useful	more useful	most useful
困難的 difficult	more difficult	most difficult
有效的 effective	more effective	most effective

(2) 不規則變化者。

原　　　　級	比　較　級	最　高　級
好的 { good / well }	better	best
壞的 { bad / ill }	worse	worst
少量的 little	less	least

多數的 many		
多量的 much	more	most
遠　的 far	farther	farthest (距離)
進一步的	further	furthest (程度)
舊的 old	older	oldest (新舊)
遲的 late	later	latest (時間)
後的	latter	last (順序)

比較的慣用句 more and more 越發，the more~，the more~，越是……越是……。no less~than 正好……，

no more than~ （=only）

(9) 冠詞 (Article)

冠詞是形容詞的一種，是冠於名詞的語，分成定冠詞，不定冠詞。

①不定冠詞 (Indefinite Article) a 與 an

a 係由 one 轉化者，在母音之前改用 an

用　　　　法	實　　　　例
ⓐ一個的(=one)	a bush, a nail, an oil pump
ⓑ種類全體的代表	A hammer is a small tool.
ⓒ每一……(單位)	once a week 每一週一次 eight hours a day 每天8小時
ⓓa＋固有名詞 (像……的……)	I will be a Ford. 我想做一個像福特那樣的人。
ⓔ個個的東西	a stone 石頭, a coal 煤塊
ⓕ以……作成的	a glass (不是玻璃而是)玻璃製的杯或鏡子。
ⓖ慣用句	as a rule 通常, on an average 平均

〔註〕ⓐ a unit（單位）。a useful metal （有用的金屬）。a European make（歐洲製）始於母音字母，但實際發音始於子音的〔ju:〕所以還是冠以 a 而不冠an.

ⓑ an hour（1小時），an honest crane man（誠實的吊車工）
都始於子音字母 h，但實際上 h 不發音而始於〔'auə〕，〔'ɔnist〕等母
音，所以冠以 an.

②**定冠詞（Definite Article）the**

the 係表示 this. that 較弱意思的語，冠於單數，複數之名詞前，在子音
前發音〔ðə〕，母音前為〔ði〕.

用　　法	實　　　　　　例
ⓐ句中已出現一次，相當於中文的"那"	Here is a valve. 這裏有一個閥。 The valve is a new type. 那閥是新型。
ⓑ種類全體的代表	The file is a useful tool. 銼刀是很有用的工具。
ⓒ從前後關係可判別者	the door 門 the machine shop 機械工廠
ⓓ用於自然物，方向等	the earth 地球，the east 東 the South pole S極
ⓔ用於計量單位名詞前	by the ton 用噸， by the kilogram 用公斤，by the week
ⓕ用於最高級	the best 最佳的，the longest 最長的， the most important 最重要的
ⓖ慣用詞	in the air 在空中，on the water 在水中， on the air 廣播中，to the right 向右側

IV.　副詞 ADVERB

副詞係說明動詞，形容詞或其他副詞的語。

　主詞　動詞　　副詞
He works hard. 他工作熱心。
　　↑＿＿＿＿｜

主詞　動詞　副詞　形容詞　名詞
It　　is a **very** easy　work. 那是非常容易的工作。

主詞　動詞　副詞　副詞
This fluorescent lamp lasts **very** long. 這螢光燈耐久。

副詞有下列 3 種。

(1) 簡單副詞 (Simple Adverb)

只用於修飾其他語句者，大部分副詞屬於此類。

It is **quite** efficent. 那是十分的有效率。

He works **very hard**. 他非常熱心的工作。

Mr. Chen finished it **exactly**. 陳先生正確的完成它，

此外尚有下列的簡單副詞。

thus, well—〔方法，狀態〕　　　enough, much, almost—〔程度，分量〕

now, then—〔時〕　　　　　here, there, nowhere, away—〔場所，方向〕

again, often, once—〔次數〕　　　why, so, therefore—〔原因，理由〕

yes, no, never—〔諾否〕

(2) 疑問副詞 (Interrogative Adverb)

表示疑問專用的副詞。

How long is this pipe? 這管有多長？〔方法〕

Where do you work in this shop? 你在這工廠的什麼地方工作？〔場所〕

When did the engine stop? 什麼時候引擎停止？〔時間〕

Why do you work so hard? 你爲什麼這樣拼命工作？〔理由〕

(3) 關係副詞 (Relative Adverbs)

連接文中語或句用的副詞。

Mount the bearing (in the manner) **how** it was mounted.

　照過去安裝的方法安裝這軸承。　　　　　　　　　　〔方法〕

Tell me (the time) **when** the launching ceremony will be held.

　告訴我午餐慶祝會將何時舉行。　　　　　　　　　　〔時間〕

This is (the place) **where** he made the boat.

　　這是他製造遊艇的地方。　　　　　　　　　　　　〔場所〕

That is (the reason) **Why** Prof. Chen approves metallic filament.

　　那是陳教授爲何認可金屬纖維的理由。　　　　　〔理由〕

關係副詞有先行詞（括弧內），但平常均省略。

(4) 副詞的比較

　　副詞與形容詞一樣有原級，比較級，最高級的變化，其用法與形容詞完全相同。

(5) 副詞的語尾

　　副詞很多時候取〔形容詞＋ly〕的形態。但語尾有稍許變化。

形　容　詞	副　　　詞	語　尾　的　變　化
swift 快的	swiftly　立刻	加上 -ly.
possible 可能的	possibly 或者	去語尾之 e，加 -ly.
heavy 重的	heavily 猛烈	去語尾之y，加 -ily.

〔註〕①下列的語並非副詞，comply 答應（動詞），apply 應用（動詞），fly 飛（動詞），飛行（名詞）。supply供給（動詞），供給（名詞）。

　　　②與形容詞同形的副詞，hard 熱心的（形容詞），拼命（副詞），long 長的（形容詞），長久（副詞），fast快的（形容詞），迅速地（副詞）。

V.　動詞 VERB

敍述有關事物之動作，狀態等的語。

Iron **is** a metal. 鐵是一種金屬。〔狀態〕

Engines **drive** machines. 引擎驅動機械。〔動作〕

動詞隨受詞之有無，分成不及物動詞與及物動詞。

ⓐ不及物動詞（Intransitive Verb）無受詞的動詞，即爲其動作，作用不影響他者。

The motor **runs** very fast. 馬達轉動很快。（very fast 是修飾語）

The car **stopped**. 汽車停止了。

ⓑ及物動詞 (Transitive Verb) 需要受詞的動詞，即爲動作除了主語以外影響到對象物。

This shop **manufactures** belts. 這工廠製造皮帶。〔受詞〕

A train **needs** rails. 火車需要車軌。〔受詞〕

(1) 受詞與補語

ⓐ受詞 (Object)——及物動詞之動作所及者（多爲名詞，代名詞），

Turbines have **runners**. 渦輪有動輪。〔名詞〕

He always does **it**. 他常作它。〔代名詞〕

ⓑ補語 (Complement)——不及物動詞有時意思不完全，又及物動詞只有受詞有時意思也不完全，此時所加語詞稱爲補語。

①不及物動詞的補語——說明主詞。〔主詞＝補語〕

This is a **nail**. 這是釘

He became a **chemist**. 他成爲化學家。

②及物動詞的補語——說明受詞

The heater keep us **warm**. 暖氣機保持我們溫暖。〔形容詞〕

They recommeded me **foreman**. 他們推荐我爲領班。〔名詞〕

(2) 根據動詞種類的五種基本句型

要素 文型	S	V	O	C
1	workers 工人們	work 工作		
2	(a) spanner 鉗子	is 是		(a small) tool. 小工具
3	Generators 發電機	generate 發生	electricity 電氣	
4	I 我	made 作	him (a)drill 給 他 (I.O) 鑽孔 機 (D.O)	
5	We 我們	elected 選爲	him 把他	foreman 領班

〔註〕 S＝主詞 (SubPect)　V＝動詞 (Verb) O＝受詞 (Object)

C＝補語 (Complement) I.D＝間接受詞 (Indirect Object)

D.O＝直接受詞 (Direct Object) 括弧內爲修飾語 (Modifier)，上表中

的 S.V.O.C. 稱爲 4 要素 (four elements)

(3) 及物動詞及不及物動詞兩用的動詞

$\begin{cases}$The siren **blew** 汽笛響了。〔不及物動詞〕

I **blew** siren 我搖響汽笛。〔及物動詞〕$\end{cases}$

$\begin{cases}$The engine **stopped.** 引擎停止了。〔不及物動詞〕

I **stopped** engine. 我停止引擎。〔及物動詞〕$\end{cases}$

(4) 修飾語 (Modifier, 略字 M)

M	S	V	M

Many scientist are studying **in this laboratory.**

很多科學家在這研究所研究着。

(5) 動詞變化 (Conjugation)

動詞有現在 (原形)，過去，過去分詞，現在分詞的 4 段變化，稱之爲動詞變化。

I **polish** the metal. 我磨光金屬。(現在)

I **polished** the metal. 我磨過金屬。(過去)

I have **polished** the metal. 我已磨完金屬。(過去分詞)

I am **polishing** the metal. 我正在磨着金屬。(現在分詞)

ⓐ規則動詞(Regular Verb) 原形＋ed 之形，但加 ed 時有時稍有語尾的變化。

現在 (原形)	過　　　去	過 去 分 詞	現 在 分 詞
finish 磨光	finished	finished	finishing
fit 裝配	fitted	fitted	fitting
couple 連結	coupled	coupled	coupling
supply 供給	supplied	supplied	supplying

ⓑ不規則動詞 (Irregular Verb) 變化上沒有一定規則者

give 供給	gave	given	giving
drive 驅動	drove	driven	driving
feed 進給	fed	fed	feeding
cut 切斷	cut	cut	cutting
run 運轉	ran	run	running

(6) 時式

動詞爲了表示對現在, 過去, 未來的狀態或動作有12種變化稱爲時式 (Tense).

ⓐ現在、過去、未來稱爲3基本時式 (Three Primary Tense).

ⓑ3基本時式與3完成時式合起來爲6時式。

ⓒ各時式又有進行式故全部合起來爲12時式。

	基　本　式	進　行　式	完　成　式	完成進行式
現在	I work	I am working	I have worked	I have been working
過去	I worked	I was working	I had worked	I had been working
未來	I shall work	I shall be working	I shall have worked	I shall have been working

①現在式 (Present Tense) 表示現在的動作狀態, 日常習慣, 不變之眞理等。

I work hard every day. 我每天努力工作。(日常之行爲, 習慣)

The earth **moves** round the sun. 地球繞行太陽。(不變之眞理)

②過去式 (Past Tense) 表示過去的動作、狀態、習慣、行爲等。

I worked hard yesterday. 我昨天努力工作過。

③未來式 (Future Tense) 表示未來的動作、狀態, 取 shall (will) ＋原形之形式。

This gauge **will pass** in the test. 這量規將通過試驗。

④進行式 (Progressive Form) 表示在現在、過去、未來的各時式動作仍在繼續進行。

⑤現在完成式 (Present Perfect Tense) 站在現在的立場叙述與過去有關連者。

現在完成＝ have (has)＋過去分詞

現在完成有下列 4 種用法。

ⓐ動作之完成:

We **have** just finished our work. 我們剛完我們的工作。

He **has done** it. 他剛作完它。

ⓑ截至現在狀態的繼續:

I **have worked** in this works these ten years.

這10年來我一直在這工廠工作。

ⓒ截至現在的經驗:

I **have** never repaired such a pump.

我未曾修理這樣的幫浦。

ⓓ過去的動作截至現在的結果:

I **have bought** a calipers (= I have the calipers now)

我已買了彎腳規。

⑥過去完成式 (Past Perfect Tense) 以 〔had ＋過去分詞〕表示而將重點置於過去。如係未來完成式 (Future perfect Tense)，以 〔shall (或 will) have ＋過去分詞〕表示，而其重點在於未來。與現在完成式一樣，各示動作，狀態的完成，繼續，經驗，結果等。

⑦現在完成進行式 (Progressive Present perfect Tense) 以 〔have been ＋現在分詞〕表示，指過去某時開始的動作連續到現在。

⑧過去完成進行式 (Progressive past Perfect Tense)，以 〔had been＋現在分詞〕表示，以過去為重點，指某一動作連續到過去之某一時刻。

⑨未來完成進行式 (Progressive Future Perfect Tense) 以 〔shall (或 Will) have been ＋現在分詞〕表示，以未來為重點，預測某一動作繼續到未來之某一時刻。

(7) 主動語態 (**Active Voice**) 與被動語態 (**Passive Voice**) 主詞主動動作的表示法為主動語態，相反的主詞的動作為被動時稱為被動語態，這兩者的區別稱為語態 (**Voice**)。同樣的文意可用主動語態或被動語態之任何一種表示。其

關係如下:

Bell **invented** the telephone

貝爾　發明了　　　電話　　《主動語態》

The telephone **was invented** by Bell

　電話　　　　　被發明　（由）貝爾《被動語態》

被動語態的作法

　ⓐ主詞與受詞位置對調。

　ⓑ被動語態的動詞取〔be＋過去分詞〕之形。

　ⓒ主動語態的主詞在被動態成爲 by 的受詞。

〔例〕We made this machine.《主動語態》

　　　This machine **was made by us.**《被動語態》

　　Carpenters **build** houses.《主動 語態》

　　Houses **are built** by carpenters《被動語態》 ⎫現在式

　　Carpenters **has built** houses.《主動語態》

　　Houses has been built by carpenters.《被動語態》⎫現在完成式

　　Carpenters are building houses.《主動語態》

　　Houses **are being built** by carpenters.《被動語態》⎫現在進行式

①有助動詞的時候

　you **must do** it. → It **must be done** by you.

　I **will punish** him. → He **shall be punished.**

②有疑問詞的時候

　What did you report? → What **was reported** by him?

③命令文的時候

　Do it at once. → Let it **be done** at once.

④否定文的時候

　I did not teach him. → He **was not taught** by me.

⑤使用器具或材料時不用 by 而用 with.

　This wall **was painted with** a brush.（器具）

This tank **is filled with** water.（材料）

⑥「從……造成」「用……造成」時使用下形。

be made of（或from）＋材料

ⓐ完成物件的原來性質未變時用 **be made of.**

This belt **is made of** leather. 這皮帶用皮革製成。

That building **is built of** concrete blocks. 那建築物用水泥塊造成。

ⓑ完成物件性質也隨着改變時用 **be made from.**

Beer **is made from** wheat 啤酒從小麥製成。

Paper **is made from** pulp. 紙從紙漿造成。

(8) 助動詞（Auxiliary Verb）

幫助動詞使意思完全的語，主要的助動詞有如下幾種。

ⓐ **do, does**（過去形 **did**）多用於疑問文，否定文。

Do you work on Sundays? No, I don't.

Did you go to the Tan-Lon Iron works this morning? Yes, I did.

ⓑ **shall**（過去形 **should**）用於未來式，表達「必須……」,「應該……」之意思。

A wire rope shall consist of 6 strands. 鋼索必須由6根絞線合成。

〔註〕should 常與 shall 同意。

ⓒ **will**（過去形 **would**）shall 同樣用於未來。表示主詞的意向，決意，有「打算……」,「想……」之意。

We will repair that oil tanker. 我們打算修理那艘油輪。

〔註〕would 常與 will 同意。

ⓓ **Can**（過去形 **could**）「能够……」,表示能力或可能性。

I can finish this work. 我能够完成這工作。

I could grind this metal. 我能研磨這金屬。

ⓔ **may**（過去形 **might**）「可以……」《許可》,「或許……」《推測》,「可能……」《可能》。

This file **may** be used. 這銼刀可以使用。（許可）

He **may** have done so. 他或許那樣做。(推測)

The calipers **may** be used as a measuring tool.

彎脚規可能使用作測定工具。(可能)

ⓕ must (過去形 had to) 強烈的「非……不可」，使用 not 則「絕不可……」，肯定的推測「一定是……」。

Must I finish this work today?

我今天非完成這件工作不可嗎？(强烈的必要)

you **must not** work till late.

你絕不可以工作太遲。(禁止)

It **must** be ture. 那一定是真的。(肯定的推測)

ⓖ have (過去形 had) 常表示完成式〔have (had)＋過去分詞〕。

Have you **finished** your work?

你完成你的工作了嗎？(現在完成)

They **had** made many V‑rocket.

他們已經完成了許多V型火箭。

ⓗ be (現在式 am, is, are: 過去式 was, were: 過去分詞式 been)「被……」之意，多用於被動語態或進行式。

This gauge should be kept clean.

這量規必須被保持清潔。(被動語態)

Those turbines **were** turning fast.

那些渦輪曾轉快着。(進行式)

(註) 以上的助動詞中 do, have, be 常用作動詞。

(9) 不定詞 (Infinitive)〔to＋動詞的原形〕

在動詞的原形之前加 to，當作名詞，形容詞，副詞使用時稱爲不定詞。

①當作名詞時

To drive a motor is not so difficult.

電動機的操作並不怎樣困難。(主詞)

I like **to design** steel towers.

我喜歡設計鐵塔。（受詞）

My wish is **to become** a chemical engineer.

我的希望是成爲一位化學工程師（補語）

②當作形容詞時

I have no meter to **repair.**

我沒有修理的量具。（形容詞）

The quickest way to **travel** is to by jet plane.

旅行最快的方法是乘噴射機。

③當作副詞時

I go to the factory **to work** every day.

每天我去工廠工作。

④被動語態的不定詞〔to be＋過去分詞〕

Iron is sent to the steel foundry **to be made** into steel.

鐵被送到鋼鐵廠煉成爲鋼。

⑤有時省略不定詞之 **to**

在 see, hear, feel, make, have, let 等主動語態的及物動詞之後，**to** 可
省略，但在被動態之後不能省略。

主　　動　　語　　態	被　　動　　語　　態
I saw the plane (to) **fly.** 我看見飛機飛翔	The plane was seen **to fly.** 飛機被看見在飛翔
I heard the siren (to) **blow.** 我聽到汽笛響了	The siren was heard **to blow** 汽笛被聽到在響

(10) 分詞 (Participle)

　　分詞係準動詞 (Verbal) 的一種，有現在分詞 (Present Participle) 與過
去分詞 (Past Participle) 之兩種形態。

①現在分詞（原形＋ ing）的用法

　ⓐ作爲進行式 (be ＋ 原形 ing)

　　A machinist **is drilling** hole on the drill press.

機械工在鑽床正在鑽孔。

ⓑ作爲形容詞

What is the **moving** stairway?

什麼是活動樓梯？

ⓒ作爲補語

You will see the high pressure line **running** across the country.

你們可以看見高壓線穿過全國各地。

ⓓ作爲分詞構句 (Participial Construction)

不用連接詞而用分詞將兩文縮成一文的形式稱爲分詞構句。遇到分詞構句時特別注意被省略的連接詞是什麼。最好考慮文的前後關係，找出認爲最適合的連接詞放進去才翻譯，分詞構句常見於工業用文章。

因爲……

Being a machine, it may break down. (= **As** it **is** a machine, it may break down.)

因爲是機器，它也許會破損。

Being gas-proof, that safety lamp requires no attention.

(= **As** it **is** gas-proof, the safety lamp requires no attention.)

因爲那安全燈是防氣，不需任何注意。

……着，……做着，而……

Saying so, he handed a handle to me.

(= **After** he said so, he handed a handle to me.)

那樣說着，他交給我操作盤。

The great heat melts the ore, **changing** it into another form of iron.

(changing = and changes)

高熱熔解着鑛石，而變成另一形狀的鐵。

當……時，

Being hardened, the steel grows hard.

(**When** the steel **is** hardened, it grows hard.)

鋼硬化時，會變硬。

如……的話

Turning to the right, you will find the dockyard.

(= **If** you **turn** to the right, you will fiind the dockyard.)

如你右彎的話，可以看到造船廠。

慣用分詞構句——也稱爲無人稱獨立分詞。

Strictly speaking, he is not a scientist.

嚴格說的話，他不是科學家。

Generally speaking, metal is heavier than wood.

一般而言，金屬比木材重。

That apprentice is very clever, **considering** his age.

從他的年齡考慮時，那見習生很聰明。

②過去分詞 (Past Participle) 的用法

ⓐ作爲被動語態 (be ＋過去分詞)

A chain **is made** of a number of links.

鏈條是由許多鏈環所組成。

A bell **is used** as a signal.

鈴被用作信號器。

ⓑ作爲形容詞

flanged pipe 附有凸緣的管——→凸緣管

welded joint 被焊接的接頭——→焊接接頭

motor-driven pump 用馬達運轉的幫浦——→馬達直連幫浦

ⓒ作爲補語

I want to have this driver **hardened.**

我要使這螺絲起子變硬。

ⓓ作爲分詞構句

(Being) **Written** in haste, this report has probably many mistakes.

(= **As** it was **written** in haste, this report ~.)

因爲寫得很忽促，這篇報告可能有很多錯誤。

Made of plastics these sheets are somewhat brittle.

因爲是塑膠製，這些薄板有一點脆弱。

(11) 動名詞 (**Gerund**) 〔原形＋ ing〕

動名詞與現在分詞同形，但是用於表達動作的名詞，工業文中常用動名詞。

ⓐ**drawing** ＝ draw (繪製) ＋ ing ＝製圖，圖面。

making ＝ make (造) ＋ ing ＝製作，製造。

forging ＝ forge (鍛煉) ＋ ing＝ 鍛造，鍛造作業。

ⓑa **floating** crane 浮着的吊車──→浮吊車 (＝a crane for floating)

a **testing** machine 作試驗的機械──→試驗機 (＝a machine for testing)

a **drafting** instrument 製圖的器具──→製圖器 (＝an instrument for drafting)

ⓒ**Wiring** is not so easy. 架線 (工程) 不那麼容易。

Television is a way of **sending** pictures.

電視是图片傳遞的一種方法。

A truck is a large automobile that is used for **carrying** heavy loads. 卡車是用於笨重貨物運輸的大形汽車。

ⓓ含有動名詞的慣用法

This works is worth **visiting** 這工廠有參觀價值。

It is no use **trying** again. 再嘗試一次也無用。

I cannot help **saying** so. 我不得不那樣說。

VI.　介系詞 PREPOSITION

置於名詞或代名詞之前，表示與其他語之關係位置的語。

The vice is fitted **on** the workbench. 老虎鉗固定在作業台上。

I went **to** the China Dockyard **at** Shiaukang **in** Kaohsiung.

我前往高雄小港的中國造船廠。

介系詞有如下兩種:

(1) 單純介系詞 (Simple Preposition)

可單獨使用者 about, above, across, after, along, among, at, before, below, beside, between, by, down, for, from, in, of, on, over, through, till (untill) to, towadr(s), under, up, upon, with, without 等。

(2) 片語介系詞 (Phrase Preposition)

由兩語以上所造成者，according to（根據～），

by means of（用～）, in regard to（關於～）

on account of（爲了～）, in spite of（不管～），

instead of（代替～）等。

(3) 片語 (Phrase)

二個以上的語連結在一起構成名詞，形容詞，副詞者稱爲片語。各分爲名詞片語，形容詞片語，副詞片語3種。

I don't know **how to read** a vernier.

我不知道游尺刻度的讀法。《名詞片語》

The punch **on the table** is his.

桌子上的衝頭是他的。《形容詞片語》

Mount this bearing **on the bearing stand.**

請把軸承裝在軸承台上。《副詞片語》

VII.　連接詞 CONJUNCTION

具有連結語與語，句與句，或子句與子句的功用，有如下三種。

(1) 等位連接詞或對等連接詞 (Co-ordinate Conjunction)

連接在對等地位的單字，片語，子句等。如 and, but, or, so, for 等。

These machines **and** electric motors are direct-coupled.

這些機械與電動機直連着。

Iron is not so ductile as copper, **but** is stronger.

鐵不如銅之有延性，但（比銅）更强硬。

The gasoline engine is used in cars, trucks **and** airplanes.

汽油引擎用於汽車，卡車及飛機。

They worked hard, **so** they finished their work at last.

他們辛苦工作，所以他們終於完成工作。

(2) 從屬連接詞 (**Subordinate Conjunction**)

連接文中的主要子句與從屬子句的連接詞，有 that, till, if, while, because.
when, though, as 等。

　　　主要子句　　　　從屬子句

I know that he is a designer.

我知道他是一個設計家。

在此例文中的 that he is a designer 具有名詞的功用，所以將此從屬子
句稱爲**名詞子句** (Noun Clause)，此外也有**形容詞子句，副詞子句**。

　　　　　從屬子句　　　主要子句

Though he worked hard, he failed.

雖然工作很勤苦，他失敗了。

　　　　　　　　從屬子句　　　　　　　　　主要子句

When petroleum is pumped out of an oil well, it is sent to a refinery.

當石油從油井抽出後，送到煉油廠。

（註）如上述從屬連接詞常冠於從屬子句之前。

(3) 關係連接詞 (**Correlative Conjunction**)

二種以上的語句互相關連連接在一起，成爲連接詞者，如 as well as (和…
…一樣)，not only~, but (also) (不但……，同時……)，so~that (非常…
…所以)，either~or (不是……，就是……)。

He is **not only** a mechanical engineer, **but** (**also**) an electrical
engineer.

他不但是機械工程師，同時又是電氣工程師。

Either you **or** I am wrong. 不是你就是我錯。

Mr. Chen is **so** skillful engineer **that** everyone in the factory trusts
him.

陳先生是非常熟練的工程師，所以工廠中的每一個人都信任他。

VIII.　感嘆詞 INTERJECTION

表達感情之語

Is that a gasoline car? **Oh, no,** it is a Diesel car.

那是汽油引擎車嗎？喔，不，那是柴油引擎車。

Well, let him do it. 好，讓他做它。

IX.　句子的種類 KINDS OF SENTENCE

(1) 由用法的分類

①敍述句 (Declarative Sentence) 單純敍述事物的句子，句尾附句號 (Period 或 Full stop)「 · 」

I can cut gear teeth. 我能切削齒輪的齒。

②疑問句 (Interrogative Sentence) 質問某一事物的句，句尾附問號 (Interrogation Mark 或 Question Mark)，動詞，助動詞或疑問詞移至句頭。

Can you cut gear teeth? 你能切削齒輪的齒嗎？

③命令句 (Imperative Sentence) 向人命令某一事物的句，句尾附句點，動詞移至句頭，但沒有主詞。

Operate this machine. 操作這機械。

④感嘆句 (Exclamatory Sentence) 表示感動之句，句尾附感嘆號（！），動詞移至句尾。

How nicely they are repaired! 修理得多麼好！

(2) 由結構的分類

①單句 (Simple Sentence) 取〔主語＋述語〕之形，句中不含子句。

A factory is a large building. 工廠是很大的建築物。

An airplane is a kind of machine. 飛機是一種機械。

②合句 (Compound Sentence) 取〔子句＋對等連接詞＋子句〕之形。

　　　　單句（子句）　　　　　單句（子句）

I worked hard **but** I failed in the test.

我努力念書但考試失敗。

(註) 子句　單句成爲合句中的一部分時，將單句稱爲子句 (Clause)。即子句雖然具備
　　　〔S＋V〕之形態但屬於句的一部分，如兩個子句並無輕重之差別，完全在對等地
　　　位時稱爲對等子句，此時用 and, or, but 等連接詞連接。

　　　片語　不像子句取〔S＋V〕之形態，只是 2 個以上的字集中形成一個意思，具有
　　　某一品詞的作用者稱爲片語 (phrase)．可分成名詞片語，形容詞片語，副詞片語
　　　3 種。

ⓐThey did not know **what to do.**

他們不知道作什麼。（名詞子句）

ⓑThat is not the right **method to do.**

那並不是應該作的正確方法。（形容詞子句）

ⓒYou must work hard **(in order) to succeed.**

你們爲了成功必須努力工作。（副詞子句）

③**複句** (Complex Senten)　由主要子句與從屬子句構成的句，其形態爲

　主要子句＋從屬連接詞＋從屬子句

　或　　　　從屬連接詞＋從屬子句＋主要子句

　　主要子句　　　連　　　從屬子句

Everybody knows that he is a hard worker.

　　連　　從屬子句　　　　主要子句

Though he is young, he is a famous inventor.

　主要子句與**從屬子句**上文中有連接詞（從屬連接詞）附在前面者稱爲從屬子
句，另一子句稱爲主要子句，從屬子句有名詞子句，形容詞子句，副詞子句三種。

　　　　　　名詞子句

ⓐ We think that he works well. 我們認爲他工作得很好。

　　　　　　形容詞子句

ⓑ I know the engineer who designed it. 我知道設計它的工程師。

副詞子句

ⓒ As you study hard, you will be an engineer.

如果你用功，你將會成為工程師。

④混句 (Mixed Sentence) 上述3種句互相結合的稱為混句。

複句　　　　　　　　　　單句

It is true that he is young, but he is a skilled plane pilot.

他年青是事實，但他是一個很熟練的飛機駕駛員。

單句

A jet plane is the fastest plane in the world,

複句

and I am not afraid of it, because it is very safe.

噴射機是世界上最快的飛機，而我並不害怕，那是因為它很安全。

X.　英文的句讀點 PUNCTUATION

(1) 句點 (Full stop 或 Period). 「．」

①附於叙述句，命令句之末。

You have a TV set. 你有電視機。(叙述句)

Finish it. 完成它。(命令句)

②縮寫字。

D.C. = Direct Current (直流)

amp. = ampere (安培)

③用於小數點。3.1416 (圓周率)

(註) 這時不稱為 Period 而讀成 decimal point 或 point.

(2) 問號 (Interrogation Mark) 「?」

附於疑問句之末。

Is that a rocket? 那是火箭嗎？

What gauge is this? 這是什麼量規？

(3) 驚嘆號 (Exclamation Mark) 「!」

附於驚嘆句之末。

What a big ship it is! 多麼大的船。

How fine this machine is! 這機械是何等的精密。

(4) 逗點 (Comma)「，」

ⓐ附於語句之間。

This works makes boilers, engines, turbines and tanks.

這工廠製造鍋爐，引擎，渦輪，和油槽。

I am not an electrician, but a mechanician.

我不是電氣工程師而是機械工程師。

ⓑ用於語句之說明。

There are two temperature scales, centigrade and fahrenheit.

有二種溫度刻度，即攝氏及華氏。

ⓒ附於數字之各第三位。

950,000 KW(KW = Kilowatt)。15,000 HP. (HP. = horse power)

(5) 引號 (Colon)「：」

ⓐ用於增加說明語句時。

Transformer: A pair of coils, usually wound on a core of magnetic material.

變壓器：普通纏繞於磁性材料磁心的一對線圈。

ⓑ用於引用別的語句時，此時再加「—」(dash).

A New York telegram says: —"Sheet steel advanced 10%"

紐約電報報導「薄鐵板漲價一成。」

(6) 分號 (Semicolon)「；」

用於比逗點大的區分時。

Clean up spilled oil immediately; it is slipping hazard.

立刻清除溢出的油，有滑倒的危險。

(7) 引用號 (Quotation Marks)「" "」

加於引用句之前後。

The old saying "Haste makes waste" is true.

諺語說「欲速則不達」是眞理。

"The extra high tension" means tension over 3,500 volts.

"超高壓"指3,500伏特以上的電壓。

(8) 省略號 (**Apostrophe**)「'」

ⓐ用於名詞之所有格。

engineer's English 工程師的英文（技術英文）。

Ohms' law 歐姆定律。

ⓑ年號，略語之略符。

'75＝1975 年　　　'phone ＝ telephone（電話）

I'm ＝ I am　　　don't ＝ do not

(9) 括弧 (**Brackets**)（　）

附於加以說明的語句前後。

Certain files (for example, the square, round, triangular files) are used for a variety of work.

某種銼刀（例如角、圓、三角銼刀）用於各種的工作。

(10) 破折號 (**Dash**)「—」

用法與括弧相同。

A mandrel — a very helpful lathe accessory — is a small tool used on the lathe work.

心軸—非常有用的車床附屬品—是用於車床工作的小工具。

The checking a micrometer should be done in the tool room — not by the machinist.

分厘卡的檢定必須在工具檢查室執行—不靠機械工。

(11) 連字號 (**Hyphen**)「-」

合成語，數字之連結之用，比破折號短。

four-cycle 四衝程, double-acting 複動式,

three-way cock 三角栓, twenty-four 24。

(12) 同上號 (Ditto)「〃」

generator for No.4 Power Station 第 4 發電廠用發電機

turbine　〃　〃　　〃　　　　〃　同上用渦輪。

2. 工業英文的語源研究——字首與字尾

英文單字的記憶在學習英文中固然重要，但由這些單字的活用再堆測未知的新單字也非常重要。工業英文的學習上特別需要說明於下面的字首與字尾的研究。

例如 side（側）之前加 in-（內）則成爲 inside（內側）；相反的加 out- 則成爲 outside（外側）。又可以推廣到 output（出力），outlet（出口），outward（外面的）等字。又如 metal 之前加 bi-（有２之意）成爲 bimetal（双層金屬），cycle（輪體）之前加 bi- 成爲 bicycle（二輪車，自行車），另外也有 binary metal（二元合金），biplane 複葉飛機等。這些造出單字的過程稱爲衍生（derivation），造出的單字稱爲衍生字（derivatives），而前面之 in-, out-, bi 等稱爲字首（prefix）。

其次以 resist（抵抗）爲例。在此單字之後加 -ant 成爲 resistant（抵抗的）即爲形容詞：加 -ance 成爲 resistance（抵抗）即爲名詞；其他如 resistible（可抵抗的），resistless（難抵抗），resistor（抵抗器），resistive（抵抗的），resistivity（抵抗力）等。以上的 -ant, -ance, -ible, -less, -or, -ive, -ivity 等稱爲字尾（suffix）。所以如果熟悉有關這些字首，字尾的知識，就可以引起「舉一反三」的作用。達到充實英文語彙的目的。

特別是在工業英文上大量的使用字首及字尾的變化，所以如果知道其規則與形式，在學習工業英文上非常方便，茲將大略的具有代表性的字首及字尾列表說明如下。

I. 字　首

含意,（ ）內爲變形	實　　　　　　　　　　　　例
ab- 反常，相反， 相對	**ab**use 濫用（ab＋use＝離正道而使用→濫用） **ab**normal 異常的。
aero- 空氣，空中， 航空（＝air）	**aero**dynamics 航空力學 **aero**plane 飛機（＝airplane）
anti- 反對的， 相對的，逆作用	**anti**friction metal 耐摩合金（anti 逆作用＋ 　friction 摩擦＝耐摩） **anti**clockwise 反時鐘方向 **anti**corrosive 防蝕 **anti**cathode 對陰極（眞空管）
auto- 自動的	**auto**car 汽車 **auto**mation 自動化 **auto**matic 自動的
bi- (bin-) 2，兩， 複，重，雙	**bi**cycle 二輪車（自行車）**bi**lateral 兩面的 **bi**nary metal 二元合金
co- (col-, com-, con-) 共，同，全	**co**operation 合作 **co**llect 收集 **com**bine 結合 **com**pany 公司 **con**centrated 集中了的
contra- 逆，反，對	**contra**clockwise 反時鐘方向（counterclockwise） **contra**flow 逆流 **contra**position 對立
deca- 10倍的	**deca**meter 公丈（10公尺） **deca**tron 10進法計數放電管
deci- 10分之一	**deci**gram 公釐（1/10公克） **deci**lites 公合（1/10公升） **deci**meter 公寸（1/10公尺）
di- 兩個的，二重的 二倍的，二分的	**di**hedral 兩面的 **di**vide 分開 **di**oxide 二氧化物
dia- 通，全	**dia**meter 直徑 **dia**metral 直徑的

dis- 反對，否定	disappear 消失（(dis=not)＋appear 出現＝消失） disadvantage 不利益 discharge 放出
electro- 電的	electroanalysis 電氣分析 electrodynamics 電氣力學
epi- 上，外	epicycloid 外擺線 epitrochoid 〃 〃
equ-, equi- 相等的	equal 相等 equivalent 等價的 equilibrium 平衡
ex-(e-, ec-, es-, ef-) 之外，全然	enormous 龐大的（e 外＋ normous 規則＝規則 　　外的，龐大的） exhaust 排出 external 外部的 eccentric 偏心的 efficiency 效率 estabish 建設
fore- 前面的，預先的， 　　領前的	foreward 前方的，前部的 foreman 領班 forepart 前部
ferro- 鐵的，含鐵的	ferroalloy 鐵合金 ferroconcrete 鋼骨水泥
hemi- 半 (＝semi)	hemisphere 半球 hemicircle 半圓
hepta-7	heptagon 七角形 (hepta7 ＋ gon……角形＝七角 形)
hexa-6	hexagon 六角形 (hexa6 ＋ gon……角形＝六角 形)
hydra- 水的， **hydro-** 氫的	hydrate 水合物 hydrogen 氫氣 hydraulics 水力學 hydrocarbon 碳化氫
hypo- 以下，以內， **hypso-** 高度	hypocy cloid 內擺線 hypsometer 測高計
in-, im-, (il-, ir-, en-, em-,) 之中，之上，使之 成為，否定	inside 內側 involve 包含 imbrown 變褐色 enclose 封入 impure 不純的 inadequate 不適當的 irregular 不規則的

inter-) 內，中，間， intro-) 相互	**inter**mediate 中間的 **inter**changeable 有互換性的 **intro**spect 內部檢查
kilo- 1,000	**kilo**meter 公里 (1,000公尺)
magni-) magna-) 大	**magni**fy 擴大，放大 **magni**fier 擴大器，增幅器
magneto- (＝magnetic) 磁性的，磁氣的	**magneto**electricity 磁電 **magneto**chemistry 磁化學
medi- 中，中等的	**medi**an 中線，中點 **medi**um 中間，媒介物
mega- 大，100萬（倍） 的（在母音之前爲 meg-)	**mega**cycle 兆週 (每一秒100萬週率) **meg**ohm 兆歐 (姆) (100萬歐姆)
met-) meta-) 改變	**met**hod 方法 **meta**morphose 變形 **meta**llurgy 冶金學
micro- ①小，微 ②100萬分之一	**micro**meter 分厘卡 **micro**farad 微法 (拉)
mis- 誤，不利，惡用	**mis**apply 錯用，惡用 **mis**calculate 計算錯誤
mono- 單獨，1 (poly 的相反詞)	**mono**rail 單軌鐵路，單軌火車 **mono**type 自動鑄字機，
multi- 多的 (＝many)	**multi**phase 多相的 **multi**tubular 多管式的
non- 無，不，非(＝not)	**non**conductor 不導體 **non**load 無負荷 **non**metal 非金屬
neo- 新 (＝new)（與原物 有關連的新物質）	**neo**n 氖燈 **neo**tric 近代的 **neo**logism 新語
octa- 8	**octa**gon 八角形 (octa 8＋gon……角形＝八角形)
out- 外	**out**side 外側 **out**flow 外流
over- 超過，過度的， 上面的	**over**flow 溢出 **over**lap 重疊 **over**load 超重 **over**heat 過熱
penta- 5	**penta**gon 五角形 **penta**hedron 五面體

per- ①完全 ②極爲 ③過（化學名詞）	perfect 完全的 perform 完成 perfervid 灼熱的 peroxide 過氧化物（過氧化氫）
peri- 回轉，周圍	periscope 潛望鏡 perimeter 周邊 period 週期
poly- 多（=many)	polygon 多角形 polyphase 多相
pre- 以前的，預先	precedent 有前例的 prevention 予防，防止
pro- 在前面	problem（pro 前面＋blem 投＝提出在前面→問題） proceed 前進 propeller 推進器
pyro- 火	pyrology 火化學 pyrometer 高溫計
quadr- quadri- quadru- 〕4	quadrant 四分圓（象限）quadruple 4 倍的 quadrilateral 四邊形
re- 〕再，返，反 red-〕（pro-的相反詞）	regress 逆行 （progress前進） rebuild 再建 reduce 還原
rear- 後部，在後方	rearheader 後管集箱 rearward 在後方
se- 離開	separate 分離 sever 切斷
semi- 半（=hemi)	semicircle 半圓 semi-steel 半淨鋼
sub- 下，次，劣等	subacid 微酸 subcontract 轉包契約 subway 地下鐵道
super- 超，優良	superior 高級的 superheat 過熱 superduralumin 超杜拉鋁
syn- (sys-, sym-)相同， 共同，類似	synchronous 同期的 symthesis 合成 system 組織，系統
tele- 遠隔，遠方	telephone 電話（tele 遠方＋ phone 說話＝電話） television 電視
thermo- 熱的	thermodynamics 熱力學 thermocouple 熱電偶

trans- 超過，移動，貫通，變化	**trans**former 變壓器（trans 變化＋former 構成物＝變形器，變壓器 **trans**porter 運搬機 **trans**piece 貫通
tri, tre, ter- 3（three 的變化）	**tri**angle 三角形 **tre**ble 三重的 **ter**nary 三元的
twi- 2，2倍的	**twi**ce 2次，2度 **twi**fold 2倍的
ultra- 超，過	**ultra**waves 超音波 **ultra**microscope 超微顯微鏡
un- ①否定 ②相反動作	**un**able 不能的 **un**balanced 不平均的 **un**gear 拆下齒輪 **un**load 卸下（重量）
under- 下，不足	**under**ground 地下 **under**cut 過熔低陷（焊接）
uni-l，單一	**uni**form 一樣的，制服 **uni**t 單位
up- 上，升	**up**grade 上坡（鐵路）**up**lift 舉高 **up**ward 向上的 **up**turned 上端彎曲的
wel-, well- 善	**well-**balanced 均衡的 **well-**paid 高薪的

II 字 尾

含意，（ ）內爲變形	實	例
-a 從希臘，拉丁文轉化的名詞複數常出現這種字尾	單數 datum maximum minimum phenomenon	複數 data 資料，數據 maxima 最大 minima 最小 phenomena 現象
-able 能⋯⋯ （**-ible, -uble**）易⋯⋯	capable 有能的力 flexible 易彎曲的	combustible 易燃的 dissoluble 可溶性的
-ace 構成名詞	furnace 爐 terrace 陽台	space 宇宙，空間

-ade (-ad, -ada, -ata) 構成名詞	arcade 拱廊　　　　myriad 1萬，巨數 strata 地層
-ae 出自拉丁文，形成名 詞複數	formula　　　　　　**formulae** 公式
-age 附在動詞變成名詞	assemblage 組立　breakage 破損 passage 通路　　percentage 百分率
-al (-ial, -ual, -ical) ①……的，關於…… ②成為名詞	general 一般的　aerial 架空式的 actual 實際的　mechanical 機械的 removal 移動　trial 試驗 manual 手册，指南
-an (ain, -ane, -ian) 形容詞，或有關「人」的 名詞	certain 確實的　artizan 工匠 mean 平均的　electrician 電氣工程師 mechanician　機械技術人員
-ance (-ancy) 造成名詞	allowance 裕度　resistance 抵抗 vacancy 空虛　buoyancy 浮力
-ant 造形容詞，名詞	assistant 助手　resistant 抵抗的 constant 常數　important 重要的
-ar 造形容詞	angular 有角的　circular 圓狀的 linear 直線的　polar 極的
-ary 造形容詞，名詞	auxiliary 補助的 rotary 回轉式的 luminary 發光體
-ate ①造動詞 ②造形容詞，名詞	accelerate 加速　calculate 計算 evaporate 蒸發 operate 操作 accurate 正確的 alternate 交互的 nitrate 硝酸鹽　sulfate 硫酸鹽
-ce **-cy** 造成名詞	once 一次　　twice 兩次 thrice 三次 efficiency 效率
-cle (-cule, -ule) 縮小或器具	particle 微片　molecule 分子 granule 細粒　vehicle 車

-craft 熟練	handicraft 手工藝	aircraft 航空術
-ee 被……的人	employee 受雇人	examinee 受驗者
-eer (-ier, -yer) 操作的人，所屬的人，機械裝置	engineer 工程師 brazier 黃銅匠 conveyer 輸送帶	glazier 玻璃工 sawyer 鋸工
-en ①形容詞，名詞之動詞化 ②名詞之形容詞化	whiten 變白 lengthen 加長 golden 像金的	heighten 增高 shorten 縮短 woolen 羊毛狀的
-ence -ency } 造抽象名詞	accidence 事故 frequency 週率	circumference 圓周 excellency 優秀性
-ent ①動詞之形容詞化 ②人，機械，作用的名詞	convenient 方便的 officient 有效的 agent 代理人	different 不同的 equivalent 等價的 current 電流
-er 表示人，機械的名詞	boiler 鍋爐 caulker 填隙機	oiler 注油器 maker 製造廠
-et (-ette, -let) 「縮小」的名詞	cabinet 小房間 turret 小塔	pamphlet 小册子 pincette 小鉗子
-fold ……倍，……重之形容詞	twofold 二倍的，双重的 manifold 多種的，多樣的	hundredfold 百倍的
-ful 充滿……， 具有……性質	bucketful 水桶滿滿的 useful 有用的	skilful 熟練的 powerful 强力的
-fy ……化， 成爲……	electify 電化 magnify 擴大	liquefy 液化 simplify 簡單化
-gen 造化學名詞	hydrogen 氫	oxygen 氧
-gon ……角形	hexagon 六角形	polygon 多角形
-i 字尾爲 -us 的拉丁文的複數	radius focus	radii 半徑 foci 焦點

-ia 拉丁外來語之語尾	ammonia 氨	magnesia 氧化鎂
-ic ①形容詞……的 ②名詞	characteristic 特有的 electric 電的 mechanic 機械工	scientific 科學的 systematic 有系統的 arithmetic 算術
-ics 表示學問的名詞	mechanics 機械學 hydraulics 水力學	dynamics 力學 electronics 電子工學
-ion (-ation,-sion,-tion, -xion) 由拉丁系動詞轉化 的抽象名詞	absorption 吸收 dimension 尺寸 connexion 連結	action 作用 adaptation 適用 (= connection)
-ior 拉丁文的比較級語尾	exterior 外的 senior 上級的	interior 內的 junior 下級的
-ize, -ise 成……,…… 化使之……	vapo(u)rize （使之）蒸發 neutrize（使之）中和	advertise（作）廣告 systematize 系統化
-ish ①……似的, 稍…… ②屬於……的	brownish 帶褐色的 greyish 帶灰色的 accomplish 完成	darkish 稍暗色的 roundish 稍帶圓形的 diminish 縮小
-ism 主義, 學說	mechanism 機構學	organism 有機體
-ist 「人」之意	chemist 化學家	scientist 科學家
-ite ①形容詞 ②名詞之字尾	opposite 相反的 ferrite 肥粒鐵	composite 合成的 austenite 沃斯田鐵
-itude 造抽象名詞	altitude 高度	magnitude 大小
-ium (eum) 拉丁文的字尾, 常見於元 素名	拉丁文 Hydrogenium Nitrogenium Carboneum	英文　　　中文 Hydrogen　氫 Nitrogen　氮 Carbon　　碳
-ive -sive } 形容詞……的, -tive } 名詞……的東西	effective 有效的 sensitive 敏感的 negative 負的	extensive 廣大的 positive 正的

詞尾	例字	例字
-l, (-el, -le) 人，器具	seal 防臭閥 chisel 鑿子	spindle 紡車軸 shovel 鏟子
-less 無……（-ful, -ous 的相反詞）	bottomless 無底的 seamless 無縫的	countless 數不清的 numberless 無限的
-like ……式，……氣	businesslike 事務式的	workmanlike 像工人的
-logy 學問，學科	rheology 流性學	technology 工藝學
-ly ①形容詞變成副詞 ②名詞變成形容詞	certainly 的確 precisely 精密的 yearly 年年的	instantly 立卽 variously 種種的 worldly 世上的
-man 造名詞「人」	boilerman 鍋爐工	workman 職工
-ment 造抽象名詞	adjustment 調節 experiment 實驗	attachment 付屬品 management 管理
-ness 形容詞變抽象名詞	brittleness 脆性 hardness 硬度	brightness 光亮度 skilfulness 熟練性
-or (-er, -ir, -o(u)r) ①表示人，器具的名詞 ②造抽象名詞	conductor 導體 reservoir 蓄水池 colo(u)r 顏色	welder 銲機 helper 助手 labo(u)r 勞動
-ory 表示場所	factory 工廠	laboratory 實驗室
-ous 充滿……，……的	advantageous 有利益的	various 種種的
-ow 名詞或形容詞	elbow 彎角	hollow 中空（的）
-ple "fold" 之意	simple 單一的	triple 三倍的，三重的
-ry ①表示動作，性質 狀態的抽象名詞 **-ery** ②表示場所的名詞	chemistry 化學 machinery 機械類，機械裝置 bakery 麵包廠	industry 工業 foundry 鑄造廠
-ship 身分，狀態	apprenticeship 見習工資格 workmanship 技能程度	

-sis 常見於希臘文轉化的單數名詞字尾	analysis basis	analyses 分析 bases　基礎
-th 由形容詞造名詞	strength 強度(＜string), length 長度(＜long) breadth 寬度(＜broad)	
-ty -ity }由形容詞造抽象名詞	safety 安全 ductility 延性	density 密度 elasticity 彈性
-um　造拉丁文系名詞字尾（複數為 -a）	maximum 最大 spectrum 光譜 vacuum 眞空	minimum 最小
-ure　表示動作，結果的抽象名詞	architecture 建築學 lecture 講義	temperature 溫度 furniture 家具
-ward(s) 方向	afterward 其後 foreward(s) 向前的	backward(s) 向後的 eastward 向東方
-ways -wise }像……向……	sideways 橫向的 broadwise 橫的	clockwise 時鐘方向 crosswise 十字狀

附　　錄

1. 美國式拼字

美國式拼字（spelling）之主要特徵為不發音的字就省略掉，所以比英國式合理得多，在下面舉例說明其大約的規則。

①把字尾由 -our 變為 -or 者

美　國　式	英　國　式	翻　譯	美　國　式	英　國　式	翻　譯
arbor	arbour	心　軸	color	colour	顏　色
harbor	harbour	港　口	labor	labour	勞　動
parlor	parlour	客　廳	vapor	vapour	蒸　氣

②兩個相同母音連續時只留其一

distil	distill	蒸　溜	carburetor	carburettor	氣化器
traveling crane	travelling crane	行走 吊車	wagon	waggon	貨　車
traveler	traveller		woolen	woollen	毛織的

③去掉字尾的 -e 者

asphalt	asphalte	瀝　青	gasolin	gasoline	汽　油
employe	employee	雇　人	gelatin	gelatine	膠

④字尾之 -re 變成 er 者

center	centre	中　心	fiber	fibre	纖　維
caliber	calibre	口　徑			
meter	metre	公　尺	liter	litre	公　升

⑤外來語之字尾變化者

catalog	catalogue	型　錄	gram	gramme	公　克
veranda	verandah	走　廊			

⑥將 -ou 的 -u省略者

mold	mould	鑄　模	molder	moulder	鑄造機

⑦將重覆的子音變成一個者

draft	draught	通　風	draftsman	draughtsman	繪圖員

⑧將ph變成 f 者

sulfate	sulphate	硫酸鹽	sulfide	sulphide	硫化物
sulfur	sulphur	硫　磺			

⑨將 y 變成 i 者

siphon	syphon	吸水管	siren	syren	汽　笛
tire	tyre	輪　胎			

⑩字尾的 -ce 變成 -se 者

license	licence	執　照	vise	vice	老虎鉗

⑪其他

fuse	fuze	保險絲	gage	gauge	量　規
gray	grey	灰　色	disk	disc	圓　盤
connection	connexion	連　結	deflection	deflexion	撓　曲

2. 美語與英語的對照比較表

美　　　語	英　　　語	譯　　文
airplane, plane	aeroplane	飛機
aluminum	aluminium	鋁
apartments	flats	公寓
ash-can	dust-can	垃圾容器
automobile, **car**	motor-car	汽車
back and **forth**	to and fro	前後
baggage	luggage	手提行李
bumper	buffer	緩衝器
can	tin	罐
coach	carriage	客車
conductor	guard	隨車員
cross-tie	sleeper	枕木
depot	station	停車場
drafting	drawing	製圖
elevator	lift	電梯
express (**train**)	non-stop train	快車
first floor	ground floor	一樓
freight	goods	貨物
gas	gasoline	汽油
hood	bonnet	車篷
intersection	street crossing	交叉口
labor union	trade union	工會
living room	sitting-room	居室
locomotive	engine	火車頭
long-distance call	trunk call	長距離電話
lumber	timber	材木
parlor	drawing-room	客廳
parlor car	salon carriage	特等客車
pavement	roadway	車路
porch	verandah	走廊
railroad	railway	鐵路

roadbed	permament way	路盤（鐵路）
sailboat	sailing-boat	帆船
schedule	time-table	預定表時間表
second floor	first floor	二樓
sidewalk	pavement (footpath)	人行道
street car	tramcar	市內電車
story	storey	樓（建築物）
street railway	tramway	市內火車
subway	underground (tube)	地下鐵道
switch	points	轉轍器
thumb-tack	drawing-pin	圖釘
toilet room	lavatory	厠所
trolley car	tramcar	市內電車
truck	lorry	卡車
wage-worker	wage-earner	薪資勞工

英語閱讀Easy Go

最完備—— 本書為全臺灣第一本最詳盡解析英語閱讀的專書。

最權威—— 全書以篇章結構理論為基礎，結合英語老師的智慧與祕訣，讓
閱讀不再是難事。

最活潑—— 新穎又淺顯易懂的解說方式，猶如專家現場指導，立即掃去對
英語閱讀的恐懼與盲點。

最容易—— 教您如何掌握文章銜接邏輯，並利用遊戲讓閱讀變得輕鬆又
Easy!

最有效—— 以大考考題作為範例，傳授高效率的解題技巧，用於升學或自
我進修皆宜。

HEAD START I、II

本套教材題材以「文化比較」為主軸,將內容延伸至聽、說、讀、寫四大層面:

1. 聽力部分:以貼近生活的對話為基礎,並以培養「全民英檢」的能力為目標,設計聽力練習。

2. 口語部分:以實際生活情境為背景,提供實用的常用語及口語練習。

3. 閱讀部分:以反覆練習的模式,導入skimming、scanning等閱讀技巧。

4. 寫作部分:深入淺出地灌輸topic sentence,irrelevance等寫作概念。

5. 內容編撰方式參考常見的文法句型及「大考中心常用7000字」,程度適中。

6. 每課最後提供Advanced Readings,全書最後並備有學習單,讓老師能夠斟酌時數及學生需要,增補上課內容。

7. 附有教師手冊、朗讀CD及電子教學投影片。

All in Reading book one、two

1. 本書以增進學生英文閱讀和理解能力為目標。課文選至國外教材,主題生活化,讀來活潑有趣。
2. 每課均有聽、說、讀、寫四大單元,讓學生均衡發展英文四大能力。
3. 版面設計採用豐富多元的照片和插圖,教學使用更活潑;標題依照四大能力分類設計,功能分類一目了然。
4. 本書並附有教師手冊、朗讀CD、電子教學投影片。

Reading plus!

1. 精選每篇約250字的英文文章共30篇，主題廣泛包含各個領域及層面，從經典文學到科學新知，從時尚購物到健康資訊，給讀者30種不一樣的閱讀感受。
2. 每篇文章附有生字表，幫助讀者理解文章內容，並增加英文字彙量；另有閱讀測驗，題型豐富多變，測試讀者閱讀技巧及理解力。
3. 附有教師手冊、朗讀CD及電子教學投影片。